Death To The Nice Guy

Vernon Wildy, Jr.

{ 1 }

"Man, that's fucked up."

A.J. stared at my cell phone in amazement as he read the text message I got from Linda McIntire last night. We had plans to go out to a local bistro for dinner but she ended up cancelling.

"So what happened with her?"

"I don't know," I replied. "I thought we were cool. We had a good time the last time we got together."

"Chris, come on. Something went down."

"I'm telling you. Nothing happened."

Then the doorbell rang. I got up from my seat and started toward the front door.

"So what did you end up doing last night?" he called out.

"Just me, the Playstation, and Madden."

"Man, you should've just gone out."

"And do what?" I answered as I made my way down the hallway. "Make up for it by getting some other girl's number?"

"Exactly!" he yelled back.

"Whatever." When I opened the door, Damon was standing there.

"What's up, man?" he said as he gave me a fist bump.

"Not much," I replied as I let him in. "I didn't know you were in town."

"Can't I surprise somebody every now and then?" We headed down the hallway to the living room.

"Hey Damon!" A.J. called out as he walked over to give him a fist bump. "Haven't seen you in the longest. What's up with you?"

"Not much, man," he replied. He took up one side of the couch as A.J. slid over to the other end. I returned to my seat on the La-Z-Boy as they got comfortable. "I don't need to come down as much since Angela moved in with me."

"So how is she doing?" I asked.

"Good, man. She's actually in town this weekend. Cousin's baby shower."

"So you're down with her?"

"Actually, she thinks I'm back in Philly. But I got something planned for her."

"Planned?"

"Oh yeah." He leaned forward in his seat. "I brought a ring down with me."

"A ring? Oh shit. Damon?"

"Yep."

"Whoa!" A.J. replied. Damon leaned back and smiled as he let the two of us take in the news.

"So you're ready to make the move," I said. "When did this happen?"

"About a couple of weeks ago," Damon answered as he stared off into space. "I looked at her and realized it was time to make it official."

"So when are you proposing?"

"Tomorrow it all goes down. But before I drop to a knee, I figure I'd have some fun tonight."

"Count me in, man," A.J. said. "Chris, you might as well roll, too."

"You already throwing me in on this?"

"After that fucked up text you got?"

"What text?" Damon asked as he turned to me. "What is he talking about?"

"Linda McIntire," I meekly answered as I sank into my seat. "We were supposed to get together last night but she cancelled at the last minute."

"Last minute? How last minute are we talking?"

"I was dressed and heading out the door. I just happened to check my phone and this popped up." I tapped a couple of buttons and then handed the phone over to Damon.

Chris,

I know we're supposed to have dinner tonight. But I don't think it's such a good idea anymore. I told you the last time I wasn't really feeling a connection with you and I still feel the same way. I know it's last minute but I think it would be a waste of time if we went out. Sorry.

"A waste of time?" Damon blurted out. He looked at me with confusion as he handed the phone back to me. "That's bullshit. You know what? A.J.'s right. That is fucked up."

"Told you," he responded.

"Well, at least she didn't hit you with the 'you're a nice guy' spin."

"I'm glad she didn't either," I said as I put my phone in my pocket. "But I wished she had said something before I got all dressed up."

Then my cell phone buzzed. I took it out of my pocket, typed in my passcode, and saw I had a text message. I tapped the message button and saw it was from Linda.

Chris,
I'm sorry about waiting so long to cancel last night. You're
a nice guy and I really shouldn't have done that. Maybe we
can still be friends.

"Get the fuck out of here," I muttered as I read her message.

"What's up?" A.J. asked.

"Linda," I replied.

"Don't tell me," Damon joked. "Don't tell me she actually did it. Did she do it?" I handed the phone back to Damon and he read the message. "Damn, she sure did. Pulled the 'let's just be friends' card after saying you were a waste of time."

"What the fuck?" A.J. replied. Damon then handed my phone to him. He read the message and started laughing.

"Now that...that's really fucked up. She's trying to play both sides of the fence on you, man."

"You know why she's doing that?" Damon asked the two of us as he took the phone back from A.J. and handed it back to me. "Because she's got the 'nice guy' label tagged to Chris' ass. Women like her keep those dudes around to fill gaps for when they're bored, lonely, broke up with their last boyfriend, or other bullshit like that. And the 'nice guys' come running, capes flapping in the air, thinking that if they save the day they'll get a shot. But there's no shot at all. A.J., had we not been here Chris would've called her."

"What?" I replied. "Come on, man."

"Chris?"

"What?"

"I know you. I know how you think, man."

"Damon...okay," I finally relented. "Maybe..."

"Told you," he said with a laugh. "Now look, before I take the plunge tomorrow, we're going out and have some crazy ass fun tonight. But I need you to do two things first."

"Two things?" I replied skeptically.

"Just trust me, okay?" he responded.

"Okay, whatever. What's the first thing?"

"Take Linda's number out of your phone."

"Do what?"

"Take her number out. Didn't she say it was a waste of time to get with her?"

"She did say that," A.J. chimed in.

"So fuck her," Damon jumped in. "Delete her ass and keep it moving."

So I slowly took my phone and tapped on the Message app and found her message. I flipped the section to the left to expose the "Delete" button, pressed and her message disappeared. Then I tapped my phone a couple of times to get to Contacts. I found her name and deleted her information from my list.

"Done," I said. "Now what?"

Damon clapped his hands and rubbed them vigorously. "Get a paper and pen."

"Do what?"

"Trust me. Just do it."

I got up from my seat and grabbed my legal pad sitting by the side of the couch. I then walked over to the kitchen to retrieve a pen.

"Get your trash can, too!" he yelled out.

"My trash can?"

"Yeah. You're gonna need that as well."

So I grabbed my trash can and brought everything out to the living room. I set the can at the edge of the table and the pen and pad at the center.

"Here's the deal," Damon began. "We did this exercise at a conference I went to last year. The speaker had us think about the things we felt were holding us back from having more success. We wrote them down, folded the paper, and then ripped it up."

"So you want me to do that?" I asked.

"Why not?" A.J. answered. "It can't hurt."

"He's right," Damon added. "This is what you need."

"I need this?" I asked.

"Yeah, you do need this. So write down 'I am a nice guy' on a piece of paper."

"Damon?"

"Just write it."

I reluctantly wrote the five words down in big letters on a page. I ripped it off from the pad and I showed him my handiwork.

"Good," Damon replied. He then pushed the pad and pen toward A.J.. "Your turn."

"Wait a minute," he replied. "You want me to do this, too."

"Hell yeah. Now think about something you could fix or get rid of."

He thought for a moment and then wrote something down on the pad. He tore off his sheet and put the pad and pen on the table.

"Okay then," Damon said as he slid up in his seat. "Now, I want you to fold your paper three times."

"Three?" I asked. "Why three?"

"The instructor said it's a magic number. Got it from a kids' song or something. Just trust me on this one."

"Three?" A.J. asked.

"Yes, A.J.," Damon replied. "Three."

A.J. and I looked at each other and shook our heads. Then we folded our pages as instructed and waited.

"Now tear your sheets into pieces."

I started to tear my sheet first. I ripped it in two and then tore it into smaller and smaller pieces before showing it to Damon. A.J. tore his sheet up right after me.

"Good," Damon said with a smile. "You've gotten rid of the thing that is keeping you from the goals you want. From now on, this thing you wrote down does not exist. Do not think about it or concentrate on it. It's now trash so throw it away."

A.J. got up from his seat and discarded his paper. I followed his action and did the same. We stood and looked at each other before laughing.

"What's so funny?" Damon asked.

"This feels crazy, man," A.J. replied as he looked at him. "We just ripped up some paper, and you're saying our lives will be better for it."

"I know it's different. But you gotta think differently these days. I know I am."

"I can tell," I said. "The fact you're talking about marriage shows that."

"I know...but that's tomorrow." Damon then jumped out of his seat and clapped his hands enthusiastically. "But tonight...we party!"

"Top Of The World?" I suggested.

"Let's do it!"

"Let me in on this," A.J. added.

"Of course you're in, man. Chris, what time we rolling over there?"

"How about eleven?"

"We can do that. But first, I need to go check into my hotel room."

"Where are you staying?"

"Omni. Top floor."

"Damn!!" A.J. replied. "You're going all out. This part of the plan?"

"Oh yeah. Gotta do it, man. But..."

"That's for tomorrow."

"You got that right. But one more thing. Chris?"

"What?" I replied.

"Make sure you take a condom."

"A condom? What the fuck are you talking about?'

"Chris, just do it. I got a feeling you'll need it tonight."

{ 2 }

Around ten thirty, I started to get dressed to go out and meet up with Damon. I thought about the exercise in the living room, of writing down I was a nice guy, of ripping up the page, and somehow things would be better. I was still having a hard time getting a grasp on that, but Damon was convinced it was going to work.

After getting dressed, I reached for my keys and wallet sitting on the dresser. As I put them in my pockets, I remembered what else Damon wanted me to bring. I had my doubts about how confident he was that I would get some tonight, but I went along with his request anyway. I headed to the bathroom and opened the closet. Sitting on the top shelf in the back corner was a box of Trojan condoms.

I had bought that box about three months ago, but it still remained sealed. I thought the occasion for opening it would've happened by now, but according to Damon, tonight was it. I opened it, ripped one off the roll, put it into the side pocket of my wallet, and put the rest away in the closet.

After securing everything in my pockets, I headed downstairs toward the front door. That's when my cell phone rang. I reached into my pocket and saw Tony was calling me.

"What's up, man?" I called out.

"Shit is crazy downtown!" he replied, trying to yell over the commotion behind him.

"What the hell's going on? I can barely hear you."

"Water main break in front of Top Of The World! Manhole cover blew up, and water's fucking everywhere!"

"What the fuck, man? When did that happen?"

"About thirty minutes ago! I was in the club, and all of a sudden...BOOM! I heard that shit and ran to the front door. Water was shooting all up in the air. Then the manhole cover came dropping out of the sky. Fucked somebody's Lexus up."

"Oh shit. So is the area shut down?"

'Hell yeah. They told everybody to get out of here."

"So where are you now?" I asked as I stepped away from the door. I walked over to the kitchen area, flipped on the light, and took a seat at the table.

"I'm a block from the club heading to my car."

"Where are you heading?"

"Paradise Lounge. They've got this hot ass adult film actress coming in as a featured dancer."

Then my phone rang again. I took it away from my ear and saw that A.J. was calling me. "Tony, hold up. A.J.'s calling." I put Tony on hold and connected to A.J.. "What's up?"

"You hear about the water main break?" he asked.

"Yeah. Tony's down there now. He said the city's shutting down the block and told everybody to get outta there."

"So what's the plan now?"

"He's going to Paradise Lounge. They've got some featured dancer there."

"Oh, Megan Allen. They were advertising that on the sports radio station all week."

"Man, I missed that one. Anyway, sounds like that's the plan."

"Cool. I'm heading out there now."

"See ya." I hung up the call with A.J. switched back to Tony. "I'm back. A.J.'s heading to Paradise now. He said the sports radio station's been pumping this all week."

"They have. New marketing guy in our building was all over that. He's stoked and so is the owner at Paradise."

"All right. Well, let me call Damon and let him know what's up."

"Damon? He's in town?"

"Yeah. He's down to surprise his girl with a ring. But he wanted to have one last night of fun before he did."

"Oh shit! My man's taking the plunge. Cool then, meet me down there."

"We're there."

"Peace."

As soon as I disconnected from Tony's call, Damon called me.

"I was about to call you," I answered.

"You hear about this damn water break. Got the street looking like a parking lot."

"Omni's two blocks from the accident. Can you get around?"

"I can get out. What are we doing?"

"Paradise Lounge. A.J. and Tony are heading there now. They told me some Megan Allen chick is the feature tonight."

"For real? She's big time in adult films. She was in Philly about a couple of years ago. Big ass billboard right on the interstate advertising her appearance. Couldn't miss it."

"Hold up, man. How come everybody knows about her but me?"

"Because you don't pay attention, mister Nice Guy."

"Oh, fuck you."

Damon broke out in laughter and then said, "Anyway, let me put Paradise Lounge on my GPS and get out there. When are you heading out?"

"Now."

"Cool. See you when you get there."

{ 3 }

With all the detours set up around the main break, it took twice as long to get to the Valley where Paradise Lounge was. Traffic moved at a snail's pace downtown as drivers impatiently switched from lane to lane to find the quickest way out. I finally got to the club parking lot, but the area was full of cars. So I ended up parking a block away.

When I walked to the front door, the last guy of a group of five was entering the establishment. At the door stood a short but stocky bald-headed guy dressed in a full tuxedo.

"Good evening, sir," he said. "I need to see your I.D.."

"No problem," I replied as I reached for my wallet. I pulled out my driver's license and handed it to him. "Seems like this is the only dry street around here."

"No joke. That water main break drove a bunch of guys down here. Place is pretty packed in there."

"I hear you," I said as he gave me back my license. "That's why I'm meeting my friends here."

"Well, enjoy yourself." He opened the door for me and I walked in.

The front area was dark except for a single lamp perched at the front cash register where the attendant sat. I paid my cover charge and walked down the corridor that led to the main stage.

The area was dimly lit, making the yellow and red patterns on the carpeted floor seem to glow. The walls were a dull red but reflected enough light to allow me to see everything around me. The stage area was anchored in the center with a metal pole connected from the stage to the ceiling. A walkway led to a pair of black curtains covering the backstage area.

I noticed the spotlight on the stage was shining on a petite redhead dancing. She was already out of her costume and was wearing white pasties over her nipples, a green G-string, and clear high heels. She danced around the pole as the guitar riffs of a heavy metal song played in the background. One of the guys at the stage dropped a few bills on the stage and she sauntered over to dance for him.

The place was crowded, but I was able to pick up where my group was sitting. They had stationed themselves at one of the tables sitting a few feet from the stage.

"About time your ass got here," Tony yelled out.

"Traffic was a bitch," I replied as I took a seat.

"Tell me about it," A.J. said. "I had to go south on 95 past the exit and work my way back up the expressway. But we're all here to celebrate."

"I know, man," Tony replied. "Damon's about to do his thing. Congrats to you, man."

"Thanks, he replied. "I appreciate that."

"You guys want anything?" a waitress interrupted as she came to our table.

"Yeah!" Tony yelled out. "Four Coors Lights and four Cherry Bombs."

"You got it, babe." The waitress left our table and headed toward another group sitting right at the stage.

"What the fuck is a Cherry Bomb?" I asked.

"Cherry Vodka and Red Bull. Trust me, shit's good. Man, we're celebrating tonight!"

"Damn, man," A.J. replied with a slight laugh. "I don't know about that one."

"You'll be all right. It's just one shot."

The dancer on stage finished her set, picked up the dollars on stage, put her dress back on, and walked through the curtains. Then the lights around the stage dimmed and sound effect blasted over the speaker.

"It's that time! Coming to the stage...tonight's featured attraction!!" the emcee belted out. A few guys got up from their seats and filled in the remaining places at the stage area as everyone else gave their loud verbal appreciation. "She's the star of film and video and twice nominated for AVN's Female Performer of the Year. Put your hands together and make some noise for MEGAN...ALLEN!!!"

Everyone gave a loud cheer as the emcee finished. Then I noticed Tony get up from his seat and applaud vigorously for the feature. He took his seat as the three of us looked at him with curious eyes.

"Oh, fuck y'all," he joked. "Like you haven't seen your fair share of porn."

"We have," Damon fired back. "But we're not cheering like you are."

"Look, this chick is bad as hell. Just watch."

"I'm watching. I'm watching."

A.J. and I just shook our heads and started laughing.

Then as the music started, a shapely brunette appeared. She was dressed in a knee-length black dress with gold patterns flowing down the center. She slinked and shimmied her way down the ramp to the center stage, lip-synching to the music, and catching the eye of random attendees. As she got to the center, she turned to our table. She went from looking sultry to pleasantly surprised. Her mouth was agape until she placed her hands gently over them. Then she snapped back into character and started her set.

A.J. poked me in the arm and leaned toward me. "Hey, she looked like she knew you."

"Yeah right," I responded sarcastically. "Megan Allen, the porn star?"

"I don't know, man. Her look..."

"I saw that, too," Damon chimed in. "She did look like she knew you from somewhere."

"Okay, guys," the waitress said as she approached our table. She had four beer bottles and four shot glasses on her tray. She sat them all down in front of the four of us and then turned to tony. "That'll be forty-five dollars."

He reached into his pocket and pulled out a stack of bills. He peeled off a few, handed them to the waitress, and said, "Keep the change."

"Thanks, babe," she replied as she put her hand on his shoulder. "You guys have fun." Then she strode away to tend to another table.

"All right," Tony said. "Everybody get a shot." We each took a glass and raised it skyward. "To Damon. I hope to God she says, 'Yes'." Laughter ensued all around the table, and then we downed our shots. It tasted really good but had a late kick to it that caught me by surprise. I took a moment to catch my breath and took a quick swig of my beer to help the shot go down.

"Man," I groaned. "That's a bit strong there."

I looked at the stage where Megan was dancing. She had pulled down the top of her dress, exposing her breasts and the gold pasties over her nipples. She spun around, facing away from the crowd, and slowly lowered the rest of her attire down to her ankles. I watched her step out of her dress and saunter over to a couple of guys who threw a bunch of bills on the stage. She danced in front of them but I saw her sneak a glance back over to my area. I thought nothing of it, figuring it was just part of her act.

{ 4 }

After her set, there was a hearty round of applause for Megan's act. She got back into her gown as the bouncer collected the bills scattered around the stage area. She then stepped off the stage and behind the curtains. The DJ made an announcement that Megan would be signing autographs and taking pictures in the private area in about fifteen minutes.

"So who's getting a picture?" Tony joked to the group.

"I don't know, Tony," I replied. "Sounds like you're asking somebody to hold your hand while you go up there."

A round of "Oooh!" came from A.J. and Damon as Tony stared at me with surprise. Then he broke out into laughter.

"Man, that's cold," he said. Then he reached out to give me a fist bump. "But that was good. I gotta give you that one."

"You were asking for that one," I replied. Then I got up from my seat and said, "I'll be back. Restroom." The guys turned their attention back to the stage to watch the next dancer take her position. I walked over to the exit area and spotted the restroom straight ahead.

"Hey," a female voice called out. I looked over to my left and there was Megan standing there, still in full costume.

"Hi," I answered as she made her way over to me. "Nice set."

"Thanks." She started to fidget with her hands and she nervously leaned on her left foot. She then took a deep breath and said, "You probably think I'm crazy but you look exactly like someone I went to high school with."

"High school? I don't know about that."

"No, I'm serious. You originally from here?"

"Richmond? No. I'm from Northern Virginia. Fairfax area."

"So am I," she replied with a smile. "Where did you go to high school?"

"John Adams."

Megan's face lit up as she covered her mouth with astonishment. "Oh my God! I went there, too!" She took a step back as she reached out to touch my arm. "Wait a minute. Did you play baseball by any chance?"

"Yeah," I answered hesitantly. "I did. Okay, this is getting a little weird."

"Crazy, isn't it? But I swear...oh goodness, now I know!" She snapped her fingers and pointed at me. "Chris Wheeler!"

Now it was my turn to stare with my mouth open in astonishment. "Um, yeah," I said, the words bumbling out of my mouth. "Uh...that's me. Well...so..."

"So who am I?" she jumped in excitedly.

"Miss Allen," a man in full black attire called out from the private dance area. "We're ready for you."

"Give me a couple minutes if you don't mind," she replied.

"Yes, ma'am."

She turned her attention back to me and asked, "You remember Mr. Perkins?"

"Yeah. I had him for Chemistry."

"You remember your lab partner?"

"Lab partner? I think so. It was… Laura…Laura…"

"Wickenshire?"

"Yeah," I replied. "That was it. But how did you…"

"Know that?" she responded with a wink and a smile.

"No way," I answered as the realization hit me square in the face. "Get the fuck out of here. Laura Wickenshire?"

"You got it."

I reached out to shake her hand but she gently slapped it away. She reached out her arms and hugged me tightly around my neck.

"It's been a while," she said as she let go of me.

"Tell me about it. But how did you…"

"It's a long story."

"Miss Allen," the man called out again.

"I'll be right there," she replied. Then she turned to me and said, "I gotta go meet my fans. But we have to catch up. Take down my number." I took out my cell phone and tapped over to Contacts. "310-555-3711. Send me a text and we'll work out when we can talk."

"Okay." I looked over to the man in black waiting impatiently for Megan. "I guess you need to be going."

"I do. But please, let's catch up." She gently placed her right hand on my left cheek before dashing off to the private area. I stood for a moment trying to comprehend what just happened. I finally made my way to the restroom, still shaking my head.

As I got back from the restroom to the main area, the DJ announced that Megan was ready to sign autographs and take pictures. I watched a few men get out of their seats while I was sitting down with the rest of the guys. Damon was making his way back from the bar. A.J. was lounged back in his seat, while Tony was finishing off his beer.

"You good, man?" Tony asked.

"I'm good," I replied. "Just watching the guys leaving to see Megan."

"I hear ya. Still not going up?"

"Nah. What am I going to do with an autograph?"

"I'm just saying..."

"Trust me. I'm good."

{ 5 }

About an hour later, I noticed everyone was losing interest. A.J. and Damon were gazing at their phones. Tony was watching some but was more intent on snagging the attention of the waitress.

"So what's up for the rest of the night?" I asked.

"Calling it a night, man," Tony replied. "My man Jake texted me and said Top Of The World is still shut down, and I don't feel like scoping out anywhere else."

"I'm with you," Damon added. "Might as well get out of here."

"Big day tomorrow," I said as I punched him in the arm.

"Yeah, man. Actually, I'm a little nervous just thinking about it."

"Man, you'll be all right." Then I finished up my beer and said, "Well, I'm gonna bounce. Tony, how much..."

"Don't worry," he interrupted. "I got y'all."

"But..."

"I got y'all."

"Okay. I'm out then." I gave a fist bump to everyone and then made my way out.

"Hey, Chris!" Damon called out as he got up from his seat. "Hold up. I'm leaving, too." He waved to everyone and followed behind me.

"Have a good evening," the lady at the front counter said.

We walked out of the club and into the parking lot. Damon's car was parked near the front, and I was in the very back of the lot.

"You good?" I asked.

"Yeah, man. Tomorrow's coming."

"I know. But you got this."

"Yeah," he replied with confidence. "I got this. I know I got this. All right, I'm out. I'll call you sometime later this weekend."

"That's cool."

I reached out to shake his hand, but instead Damon reached out and wrapped me into a tight hug. It caught me by surprise for a moment, but I hugged him back.

"Thanks," he said. "Thanks for being there."

"No problem, man. I go too far back with you not to. Now go do your thing tomorrow."

"No doubt." He made his way to his car, threw up a peace sign to me, and drove off the lot.

As I walked toward my car, I took out my phone and found the number Laura gave me. Then I sent her a quick text.

Hey Laura. It's Chris. Great running into you. A little unusual but it was good. Hope to catch up with you soon.

I put my phone back in my pocket as I got to my car. Just as I opened the door, my phone buzzed. I pulled it out and saw that Laura was calling me back.

"Hey," I said.

"Hey yourself. Still at the club?"

"Yeah, but I'm about to leave. The guys are calling it a night. What's up with you?"

"Back at the hotel. Figured I'd answer some e-mails before bed but..."

"But what?"

"Just thinking about tonight. Seeing you...at that place... just nuts."

"Small world, isn't it?" I joked.

"Hey," she inquired. "You got time to stop by?"

"Sure. Where are you?"

"Marriott Downtown."

"Oh yeah," I answered assuredly. "You're a few blocks up Broad. I can run by there. What room?"

"Four fifteen."

"Okay. See you in a bit."

"See ya."

I put my phone back into my pocket and shook my head. "This is crazy," I muttered to myself. I pulled out of the lot and drove up Broad to the hotel. I parked across the street and then made my way to the hotel lobby. I walked in and saw the front counter attendants busy with a group of people checking in. I strolled by them and went to the elevator. I rode up to the fourth floor and made my way to her room.

"Hey!" a voice called out as I got to her room. "What the hell you doing up here?"

I looked over and saw a rather burly dude dressed in all black Nike gear quickly coming my way. The look on his face indicated he wasn't too keen on me being there.

"Um…" I tried to explain. "I'm here to see…Laura…um, Megan…"

"Laura?" he stopped me. Then his mood lightened up. "Oh, you must be Chris."

"Yeah," I answered hesitantly. "Chris…Chris Wheeler."

"She said you were coming, probably refer to her by her real name." He reached out to shake my hand. "Sorry I came at you like that. Just doing my job."

"No problem," I replied. "So you're security?"

"Yeah. Luther Mathis, Mathis Security. I watch her back when she's on the East Coast." Then he started laughing. "You and her? High school? That's some crazy ass shit, man." He gave me another lookover before gong back to his room, laughing harder than before.

I turned my attention back to her door. I stood there for a second to collect myself and then knocked on the door. Almost immediately Laura opened it. She was dressed in a T-shirt and shorts, smiling as she stood in the doorway. Her hair was in a ponytail and she was wearing glasses.

"Chris! You made it. Come on in."

"Good to see you," I responded as I walked in. "I think…"

"You ran into Luther, didn't you? I told him you were coming."

"Big guy," I replied. "Means business, too."

We walked down the short hallway to the bedroom. A queen-sized bed sat in the middle of the room with a lamp stationed at each side. A table with two chairs sat in the far corner and a drawer set and TV sat across from the bed. Her suitcase was against the wall next to it and few clothes were tossed around the floor.

I started to make my way toward the bed when Laura gently grabbed my hand. "Hold up," she said. "Now that I'm not in a rush, let me take a look at you." She looked me over and smiled. "You haven't changed one bit."

"Thanks," I responded. "But you...now that you're wearing glasses, you definitely look like my lab partner." She giggled as she hid her mouth with her hands. "But...

"I know. It's been a while."

"It has."

"Now enough staring at each other. Sit down, and let's catch up." She hopped on the bed and sat cross-legged on the right side. I walked over to the left, took my shoes off, and reclined myself resting on the headboard.

"So," I started. "I have to ask..."

"How did Laura Wickenshire from John Adams High School become Megan Allen, porn star?"

"Yeah. I guess we can start there."

She laughed slightly as she ran her hand through her hair. "It's crazy, really. I got my bachelor's from George Mason, and I had every thought of going to grad school. But I decided to take a year off from school and just do whatever.

That's when Alicia Brooks talked me into going out to California with her."

"Oh, I remember Alicia. You two were tight at Adams."

"Still are. She's in Denver now, married with three kids. Next time I talk to her, I'll tell her I saw you."

"Cool. But I know your parents probably freaked out when you brought up California?"

"My mom wasn't too thrilled, but my dad was okay with it. She finally relented after he mentioned all the trips she used to make down to Georgia to see him in college and how it drove her parents crazy. So Alicia and I drove west, found a place to live, got jobs, and enjoyed the sunshine."

"So how did you end up in adult entertainment?

"It all started with a dare. We dared each other to enter an amateur dance contest at a local strip club."

"And let me guess? You won."

"You got it. The owner of the club liked what he saw and offered me a chance to dance as a regular. So I decided to go for it. Made some good money, too. After the year was about up, I was thinking about grad school again. But then I met a couple of girls in the industry at a party, and they introduced me to their agent."

"Next thing you know..."

"Doing photo shoots, then softcore scenes, and then... you know the rest."

"So much for school?"

"I'm actually doing that, too," she replied with assurance. "Taking online courses from UCLA, business management."

"Business management?"

"Got to. I've got films, custom videos, a website, merchandise, feature dancing, and appearances to take care of. Chris, I'm running a business, babe."

"I see," I replied as I nodded my head. "My Chemistry lab partner. The same girl who never wore a skirt to school."

She tilted her head back and laughed out loud. "I know!" she replied. "The only time I wore a dress was prom and graduation."

"And now look at you? Showing it all off."

"You're funny." She sat silently for a moment, looking away but I could tell she was still smiling from that last statement. She turned to me and asked, "So what about you, lab partner? What's your story?"

"I did what everybody else did," I replied as I shrugged my shoulders. "I went to college, got my degree, worked in a couple different cities, and ended up in Richmond. I'm now working for a major electronics store chain in human resources."

"Married? Kids?"

"Nope."

"That's a shame."

"Why?'

"You're a really great guy."

We gazed at each other in silence. Then she reached out her hands and grasped on to one of mine. She slid closer to me as she caressed it.

"I could've made you happy," she said as she gently kissed my index finger.

"You could've what?" I quietly replied. "What are you talking about?"

"You know, so much is coming back to me sitting here with you."

"Coming back? Okay Laura, what's going on?"

She looked down at my hand as she caressed it over and over. Then she took a deep breath as she looked up at me. She was about to speak but instead nervously bit her lower lip.

"Chris," she finally said. "I have a confession."

"A confession?"

"Yeah. You game?"

"Sure," I replied. "Why not? Lay it on me."

"Well," she said slowly. "I...I had a major crush on you in high school."

"Whoa!" I responded as I sat further up. "I didn't see that coming. You?"

"Yeah. I did." She gripped my hand tighter and held it to her chest. "You know, I actually looked forward to Chemistry class, even if Mr. Perkins was a jerk."

"He wasn't a jerk all the time. He did have his days but..."

"Chris, you never let him get to you. And I knew when you there, I'd be okay."

I took a deep breath and then said, "Wow. This is getting heavy."

"I know," she replied as she held my hand in her right and rubbed my forearm with her left. "I never had the chance to tell you. You were so smart and confident. Plus, I really thought you were hot."

"What? Wait a minute. Why didn't you…"

"Chris, I was scared," she said as she let go of my hand. "I didn't think you would like me."

"Laura…"

"You were a jock; you were smart, popular…" She looked away to hide her face. I could tell she was blushing a little embarrassed.

"Laura?" I asked. "What are you thinking?"

"Promise you won't laugh if I tell you something else?"

"Something else? There's more?"

"Yeah. There is."

"Well, go for it."

She slid closer and sat on her knees. She smiled at me as she took a couple of deep breaths to compose herself.

"Okay," she said. "Do you remember your forty-game losing streak?"

I laughed out loud and then replied, "Oh yeah. How could I forget?"

"Well, when you guys finally won…I thought about doing something for you."

"Doing something?" I asked.

She nodded her head as she pushed a strand of hair away from her face. "I know it sounds crazy and I talked myself out of it because I thought it was crazy and I didn't want you to think I was crazy and…"

"Laura," I interrupted. "I never thought you were crazy. Besides, whatever you were thinking about would've been a hell of a lot better than Coach Abraham's speech after the game." I patted her on the thigh and said, "So tell me. What did you want to do?"

She crawled toward me and placed a hand by my neck. Then she pulled herself close and kissed me. The action caught me by surprise, but I returned her advance and kissed her back. Our lips stayed locked for a few seconds before she slowly backed off. She straddled herself across my crotch as I maneuvered myself to sit higher on the bed to where we were eye to eye. She wrapped her arms around me and kissed me deeper.

As our mouths locked, I could feel her hands rubbing the back of my head and then toward my ears and temples. My hands drifted down to the small of her back and then inside her shirt. I unlocked my lips from hers and began to kiss her neck, causing her to tilt her head back and moan ever so. I explored her body from her back, around her torso, and then to her breasts. Sensing where my hands were, Laura removed her shirt.

"Nice," I whispered.

"You like?"

"I do."

I gently squeezed her left breast before putting a nipple into my mouth. She moaned into my ear and kissed my earlobe as I sucked and nibbled on her nipple.

"You got too many clothes on," she cooed as she pressed her forehead to mine, tugging at the shoulders. I reached me arms skyward as she pulled off my shirt. She then slinked her way down my body, gently kissing her way down my neck and chest until she got to my belt buckle. She then rose up on her knees as she fumbled with my belt and pants.

"Wow," I replied as she pulled off my pants.

"Sounds like you never had someone strip you naked before," she said as she stepped off the bed.

"Can't say that I have. But all of this for a baseball game?"

"Of course not, silly," she said as she took off my socks. "We were kids then." Then she reached for my boxer briefs and slid them off. She took a moment to review my naked body before slipping off her shorts and panties. As she crawled back onto the bed, she took my erection in her hand. "We get to play adult games now."

Before I could respond, she placed her index finger to my lips. She reached over my head to grab a pillow, set it behind me, and gently guided me to lay back. Then she slid down my body until her head was below my crotch. She slowly stroked me as she alternated kisses to each of my inner thighs.

Then I felt her mouth caress my balls. I moaned as the feeling of her down there sent shockwaves through my body. She then kissed her way up the shaft of my dick until she got to the tip. I lifted my head up to look at her. She looked back and winked at me as she gave the tip a gentle kiss. She then took me into her mouth, and it made me fall back into the pillow. She mixed up her speed and how far down she went while gently raking her nails along my chest down to my thighs.

"You are so hard," she panted. Then I heard her say something else that I couldn't pick up.

"What?" I responded as I lifted my head up.

"I wouldn't mind having this inside me," she whispered.

"Well..." I tried to answer. But when she took me deep into her mouth once more, I fell back into the pillow.

Then in a moment of clarity, I remembered the condom in my wallet.

"Wait a minute," I said. I sat up and tapped Laura on the shoulder. She looked confused for a moment but then slid off to the side while I climbed off to look for my pants. I fumbled through my pockets and grabbed my wallet. I unfolded it and reached in the liner to find the condom. I turned to face Laura at the edge of the bed. Seeing what I had revealed, she smiled as I returned to the edge of the bed.

"Nice," she said as she gently stroked me. "Now put that on. I want you to fuck me."

{ 6 }

My eyes popped wide open around seven in the morning. I was in bed staring at the ceiling and then the surroundings of the hotel room. It all seemed as if I didn't belong there. But then I felt Laura snuggle up tighter against me. I looked over and saw she was still asleep, my arm wrapped around her shoulder as she rested her head at my side and her arm on my chest. I sunk my head back into the pillow and tried to go back to sleep.

But I woke back up about twenty minutes later, just as wide eyed as before. This time I could feel Laura move about under my arm. I looked down and watched her placed her head directly on my chest. She wiped her hair from her face, looked up at me, and smiled. Then she leaned toward me for a kiss.

"Good morning, baby," she whispered. "You're up early."

"Morning to you," I responded. "You're up early, too." I took a deep breath and stretched out my free arm. "What a night."

"Tell me about it." She leaned in and kissed me again, deeper and longer than the first. "You were great last night."

"Great?"

"Oh my God, yes. Sex with you was wonderful."

"Come on, Laura…"

"Yes, really," she replied as she put a finger to my lips to hush me. "You felt so good inside me." She smiled as she pulled her finger away and ran it in tiny circles on my chest. "You know, I dreamed about us last night."

"About us? Let me guess. Chemistry class?"

"Oh yeah."

"That's funny." Then I broke out an impersonation of our teacher. "Now Wheeler and Wickenshire. Let's make sure we don't break anything else when we do our experiments."

"We only broke one beaker."

"We broke two. And a test tube."

"A test…oh God!" she replied as she broke out in laughter. "Now I remember the test tube. Too funny." She pushed back the covers and rolled over on her stomach. "Can I tell you something?"

"Oh no," I joked. "What other surprises you got for me?"

"It's not like that. It's just that…outside of my parents, you're the only person who calls me Laura."

"You don't like being Megan?"

"I'm not saying that at all. I'm Megan to the world and in many, many fantasies. But I'm still a real person. So it was nice to be Laura last night, especially to my high school crush."

"It was good to see you, too," I said as I turned a strand of hair away from her face. "But you gotta take care of Megan."

"Oh yeah," she replied as she rested her head on my chest. "I've got a meeting with my agent on Tuesday. Book my scenes, set up photo shoots for my website, and set up another set of features and appearances." Then she rose up and inched her way toward me. She kissed me and said, "I don't want to think about that right now. My flight's not until two and I told Luther he could sleep in."

"So what's on your mind?"

"This was an unexpected surprise, and I'd like to enjoy it for the rest of the morning." She then rolled out of bed as I rose up into a seated position. "I still can't believe I saw you in the crowd last night."

"Be honest," I replied. "How fast did you recognize me?"

"Immediately," she answered as she grabbed the hotel menu from the TV desk. "You have not changed since high school, and your face just stood out. I kept looking back at you through the whole set because I thought it was a crazy coincidence. Then I saw you out in the hall and..."

"The rest is history?"

"You got it. I did want to catch up with you, and we surely couldn't do it in the club. But when the moment arises, you gotta roll with it." She then turned her attention to the menu. "So what do you want for breakfast?"

"Do they have pancakes?" I inquired.

"Sure do."

"Cool. Let me have that, some sausage, and orange juice."

"Got it."

As she picked up the phone, I got out of bed and made me way to the bathroom. I looked around at the curling irons, hair care accessories, and makeup taking up most of the space on the dark brown sink counter. I raised the seat of the toilet and relieved myself. Then I looked up at the reflection of myself in the mirror.

"What a fucking night," I whispered to myself.

I finished up, flushed the toilet, washed my hands, and made my way out of the bedroom. Laura was standing there with a sly smile on her face.

"We have thirty minutes until breakfast comes up," she said as she slowly approached me. She wrapped her arms around my neck and kissed me.

"What are you up to?" I asked.

"I told you I wanted to enjoy the rest of the morning." She kissed me again, this time slow and deep as she pressed herself against my body. Then she hopped up and wrapped her legs around my waist. We continued to kiss as I carried her to the bed. When I laid her down, she unwrapped herself from me and left herself open for my advances. I leaned in and sucked on one of her nipples, making her exhale as my mouth touched her skin. I kissed my way down her body until I made my way in between her thighs. Then she gasped as my tongue touched the lips of her pussy.

"Oh, that's good," she moaned. "That's so good, baby."

I took turns sucking and licking her as her moans and breaths intensified. Then I felt her hands caress my head, guiding me in farther. I felt her body tense up and her breaths become more hurried. Then she went silent for a few moments before letting out a guttural moan as she went into orgasm. Finally, she pulled my face away and guided me to where she was in a sitting position.

"Fuck," she said out of breath as she pressed her forehead to mine. "Damn, that was awesome." She kissed me and collapsed on the bed. I lay down on top of her, and we made out.

Then there was a knock on the door.

"That's probably breakfast," she said. "Want to get that?"

"Sure."

I got off of her and looked for something to cover myself. Laura climbed under the covers, still trying to catch her breath.

{ 7 }

After breakfast, a shower, and an amazing goodbye blow-job from Laura, I staggered out of the hotel around eleven and headed home. My mind was racing, trying to digest the events of last night. As I got to my car, I took a long look at the hotel before driving off to go home.

When I arrived, I saw a car pull in right behind me in my driveway. The sight caught me by surprise, and I quickly jumped out of my car. But then I relaxed because I saw it was Tim that had pulled in behind me. I had barely seen him since he and his wife were expecting their first child any day now.

"What's going on, man?" I called out.

"Not much," he responded. We gave each other a fist bump and started walking toward the front door. "Mother-in-law's in town and she's giving me a break. So I figured I'd hang out with my boy." He plucked at my shirt sleeve and said, "Looks like you've been out all night."

"You have no idea," I replied as I opened the door. Tim walked in ahead of me and down the hallway while I stepped in and closed the door. "You want anything?"

"Beer's cool," he called out.

I went to the fridge and got a beer and a bottle of water. I went to the living room, handed him the beer, and sat down on the La-z-boyy.

"Just water?" he asked, surprised at my choice.

"That kind of night."

"Good or bad?"

I gave him a thumbs-up as I was drinking my water. The look on Tim's face was one of curiosity, and I figured I may have to tell a little more. That's when my cell phone rang. I saw that it was Damon on the other line. I responded to his call and put him on speakerphone.

"Damon, what's up?" I answered.

"She said yes!"

"All right! Congrats!"

"What?" Tim called out. "Someone's about to get married?"

"Who's that?" Damon asked.

"Tim's over here," I said as I moved from my seat over to the couch. I sat the phone down on the coffee table between the two of us.

"What's up, Tim?" Damon said.

"Not much, man. So you're going for it, huh?"

"Yeah, man. I came down yesterday to get things straight for today. Hung out with Chris and the crew last night before having to do my thing."

"Looking at Chris, I can tell you had fun."

"What are you talking about?"

"I just got home," I said after finishing off the bottle of water.

"You just got home? What the fuck did you do last night?"

"Damon, you wouldn't believe me if I told you."

"Try me. How crazy could it possibly be?"

Then the doorbell rang. "Give me a sec." I got up and headed to the front door. When I opened it, A.J. came rushing in with a manila envelope in his hand. He walked briskly past me and straight to the living room.

"Tim!" he said. "What's up, man? I haven't seen you in a minute."

"Getting ready for fatherhood, my man," he replied as he gave him a fist bump.

"Who's that?" Damon called out on the phone.

"That's A.J.," I replied as I stood over everyone.

"What's up, A.J.? It's Damon."

"What's up, man," he replied. "I hope she said yes."

"She did. She's outside the door right now calling people and texting pictures of the ring. But enough about that. Have you seen Chris?"

"Yeah, man," he said as he observed me. "You still wearing your shit from last night?"

"Yes, I'm still my wearing my shit from last night," I answered begrudgingly.

"What the fuck happened?"

There was a moment of silence as A.J. and Tim were intently looking at me for a story. Feeling the pressure, I took a seat between them on the couch and set the phone directly in front of me.

"Remember the feature dancer at Paradise Lounge?"

"Megan Allen, right?" Damon responded.

"Yeah. Well, I ran into her in the lobby after her set. We realized we knew each other."

"Knew each other?" Tim asked. "From where?"

"High school."

"High school?" A.J. replied. "You went to high school with Megan Allen?"

"Yeah, we went to high school together. We met up afterwards at her hotel room to catch up."

"Wait a minute. Catch up on what?"

"Hold up," Tim jumped in. "Who the fuck is Megan Allen?"

"Hand me my laptop. It's by the edge of the couch." Tim reached over and grabbed my laptop. I turned it on, went online, and pulled up Megan's Twitter feed. "That's Megan."

He took a look at her pictures and then back at me, impressed by what he saw. "You went to high school with her? Damn!"

"Okay, okay," Damon butted in. "Let's get back to the catching up part. That sounds nice, but..."

"Damon, no," I said.

"Chris?"

"Come on, man."

"Look..."

Then my phone buzzed and beeped, signaling a text message had come up. It was from Laura and the message popped up in the upper portion of the display. Tim picked up on it and snatched the phone away from the group.

"Will you give me that?" I asked in a raised voice. "That's for me."

"Who's Laura?" Tim inquired.

"Laura?" Damon called out. "I thought we were talking about Megan."

"Give me my phone!" I replied bluntly to Tim. I grabbed his arm and pulled my phone from his grasp. I took a look at the display and Laura's message.

Hey, it's Laura. I'm at the airport heading back to CA. I had an amazing night with you and I'm glad we got to catch up. Do me a favor. Please don't post anything about you fucking Megan Allen. Let's keep that between us. Thanks, babe. Keep in touch.

I tapped the phone to turn the message off. I looked up and saw A.J. and Tim waiting for an explanation.

"Look," I finally relented. "This shit stays here."

"No doubt, man," Tim said.

"We got you," A.J. added.

"You got it," Damon responded. "You know us, man."

"Here's the deal," I started. "Megan's real name is Laura and we went to high school together. After graduation, we went our separate ways. She went to college and instead of going to grad school, she went to kick it in California for a year. I won't get into details but one thing led to another and she's now well known in the industry. She was at Paradise Lounge and she recognized me. She invited me back to her room, we caught up on old times, and then..."

"You fucked her," Tim cut in.

"You weren't supposed to have read that."

"Wait a minute," Damon said. "You fucked Megan Allen?"

"Damon..."

"Damn!" A.J. cut in. "That's crazy, man."

"Chris," Damon added. "Do you know what you've done? Do you understand what you just accomplished? There are guys out there jerking off to a Megan Allen video right now, fantasizing about what it would be like to be with her. And you got to fuck her for real."

"Come on, Damon," I tried to explain. "This is Laura from my high school."

"Laura...Megan...who gives a shit?" Then I could hear a female voice in the background call for him. "Okay, I'll be there in a second. What...I'm talking to Chris...just told him." Then he returned to his attention back to me. "Angela says hello. But anyway, you got to ride this momentum."

"Momentum? What?"

"Yes! Momentum. You got something going here, man. Now you've got to get back out there and be more public. You can't sit on your laurels now. Look, I gotta go. But Chris, you did damn good. Keep it going."

"Okay. Whatever."

"Keep it going!"

"Okay, okay. Tell Angela I said congrats."

"I will. Out."

Damon hung up the phone, and I disconnected on my end. I picked up my phone, put it in my pocket, and moved back to my Lay-Z-Boy to sit down. I looked over at A.J. and Tim, and they were staring at me with shit-eating grins on their faces.

"What?" I asked.

"You fucked a porn star," Tim said with a snicker. "Damn, I'm proud of you."

"Oh, shut up." I then turned to A.J. and asked, "So what's in the envelope?"

"*River City Magazine* is putting together a fantasy baseball league and doing a story about it," he said as he held up the envelope. "They picked Tony, and he got me in. Twelve-person league but somebody dropped out at the last minute, so I'd figured..."

"He'll be there," Tim answered.

"What?" I gasped. "You're my spokesperson now. A.J., when is the draft?"

"Tonight. Seven-thirty."

"Tonight?"

"Don't worry. He's in," Tim cut in again.

"What?"

"You're in."

"Okay, okay," I finally relented. "I'm in. Where's the draft?"

"Bailey's Tavern. Make sure you bring your laptop."

"I'll do it." Then I turned to Tim and asked, "What are you doing to me?"

"Hey, man. Momentum. Keep it going."

{ 8 }

A.J. and Tim left soon afterward and I tried to get some resemblance of a nap. But after thirty minutes of tossing and turning, I gave up. I took a shower, got dressed, fixed myself a sandwich, and headed out to the bookstore.

When I got to Broad Street Bookstore, I made my way to the magazine racks. I was casually flipping through the preseason baseball magazines when I heard a female voice come over the intercom.

Attention bookstore shoppers. Would Chris Wheeler please come to the Information Desk? Chris Wheeler, please come to the Information Desk.

The announcement caught me by total surprise. The only person I really talked to in this place was Stacie, and she was now in Florida. As I made my way over, I was trying to figure out who would ask for me.

When I got there, the only person I saw was a short woman wearing her black hair pinned back. She wore an unremarkable blue blouse and gray full-length skirt. She also wore glasses but they were perched on top of her head.

"Excuse me," I said. "I'm Chris Wheeler. Did someone call for me?"

The woman looked up and took a good look at me. Then she pulled out a piece of paper with a photo attached to it. After looking at it, she turned her attention back to me and smiled.

"Hi, Chris," she said as she eagerly extended her hand. "I'm Lydia Alston, the new events coordinator. Nice to meet you."

"Nice to meet you, too," I responded. I reached out to shake her hand, still wondering why she called me out of the blue. "How..."

"How did I know who you were? Stacie left me a note. Here, take a look." She handed me the note and a picture of me at the last Christmas party.

Lydia,

I hope things are going well at the bookstore. I want you to meet this guy that comes by there. His name is Chris Wheeler, and he is an absolute sweetheart. He'll always claim that he stays busy but he's well worth the effort to get him to your programs.

    Take care of the place,
    Stacie

"Wow," I responded in surprise. "She left a note about me?"

"She still thinks the world of you. In fact, she e-mailed me this morning to see if we've met."

"Well, we've met," I kidded. "So I guess now you'll be nagging me to death about coming to your programs. But..."

"You stay busy?" she responded. "I've been warned you would say that. But I already know how to get to you." Then she handed me a pamphlet. "We've setting up a new online mailing list. So you better sign up."

"I better?"

"Yes, you better," she replied with a sly smile. "Or else."

"Or else what?"

"I'll have to come out and find you," she said as she playfully shook her finger at me.

I laughed and then said, "Uh oh. I'm already in trouble. Okay. I'll do it when I get home."

"Good deal." Then a guy with long blond hair and a bushy beard came to the Information Desk, looking over the Current Events section. "I have to go. See you soon?'

"I'll be around. Nice meeting you, Lydia."

"You too. Take care." She then headed over to tend to the guy standing at the desk.

"Hey Chris," a male voice called out. I looked back toward the front door, and I saw it was Tony. He strolled toward me and quickly glanced at the magazine I had in my hand.

"Somebody's getting ready for a draft," he said.

"Yeah," I replied. "Got talked into a draft at the last minute."

"I feel you. I haven't had a chance to look at anything. And I got a draft tonight. So when is yours?"

"Mine's tonight as well."

"Wait a minute. *River City Magazine* by any chance?"

"Yeah. You're in that, too?"

"Oh yeah," he responded as he snapped his fingers. "That's right. A.J. said he was gonna try to get you in." But then his attention turned to the Information Desk. "So, who was that you were talking to?"

"Oh, her," I answered as I looked over in Lydia's direction. "Someone who used to work here told her to look out for me. She's had a note about me for a while."

"What?" he replied as he turned to me. "Man, you got some karma going on. Got women sending messages to look out for you?"

"I don't think it's like that. But...shit has gotten crazy all of a sudden."

"What do you mean by that?"

I started to answer but instead motioned him over to the corner of the store by the front window.

"Last night at Paradise," I said.

"What about last night?"

"You remember the feature dancer?"

"Megan Allen? Shit, yeah."

I leaned in and said softly, "She and I went to high school together."

"Get the fuck…" Tony started laughing but then realized I was telling the truth. He then looked at me with shock on his face. "Get out of here. That's crazy, man."

Then I hesitantly added, "That's not all."

"Wait a minute. What else happened?"

"We got together afterward at her hotel room and caught up on old times. Then…"

"Oh shit," he whispered. "Oh shit! Did you…"

"Tony!" I said as I put my index finger to my mouth. I could see behind him a couple and their small child walking toward the magazine section. But then they veered away to another part of the store. "Dude, you can't say a thing."

"No problem, Chris. But still…"

"Still what?"

He leaned in and whispered, "You fucked her, didn't you?"

"Yeah, I did."

"Oh shit!" he replied as he tried to keep his excitement down. He slapped my arm and said, "You a bad man, Chris."

"Come on, Tony. It's not like that. She and I were cool in high school. I had no idea that was going to go down."

"It doesn't matter," he responded as he clapped the back of his right hand into his left palm. "You fucked her. You did something that most men fantasize about. Look at you. You've got the power of attraction on your side."

"Come on, man."

"I just saw the way the other one at the counter was looking at you."

"Tony, you're going too far," I said, trying to calm down his enthusiasm.

"Am I?"

"Look," I replied as I looked at my watch. "I gotta go. I'll see you tonight."

As I started toward the front counter, Tony called out, "All right, man. But you better get an umbrella."

"Why?" I replied as I turned back to him.

He walked up to me and whispered, "Because women are about to fall on your head like rain." He then slapped my shoulder twice and walked off.

{ 9 }

I got to Bailey's Tavern that night and asked the waitress where the fantasy group was meeting. She pointed me to a room in the back, and I headed that way. When I got there, a sign on the door indicated the room was reserved for *River City Magazine*. I walked in and saw a group of people sitting around a table, each with their laptop open. A.J. and Tony spotted me and waved me over to the empty seat next to them. Then I was greeted by a woman wearing a Cardinals hat and T-shirt along with blue jeans and sneakers. She was almost as tall as I was, and her brown eyes shined as much as her smile.

"I take it you're Chris," she said warmly as she reached out to shake my hand.

"That would be me," I replied as I shook her hand.

"Awesome. I'm Danny Walker with *River City Magazine*. Thank you so much for participating."

"Thanks for having me. But I have to ask you..."

"Danny," she replied with a smile. "Short story...Dad wanted a boy but ended up with a houseful of girls." Then she lightly tapped me on the arm. "I'll have to tell you the long story later. Go ahead and grab a seat because we're going to get started real soon."

"Sounds good," I replied. As I walked away to the empty seat, she gave me a slight tap to my lower back.

"What's going on, Big Smooth?" Tony joked as I took a seat next to him. Then he leaned in and whispered, "You got it going on, man."

"What are you talking about?" I replied.

"I saw the way she looked at you. The way she kept tapping your arm and stuff."

"Come on, man," I said as I took out my laptop. "She's just being friendly."

"Friendly? Right. Just remember...like rain."

"Will you stop it?"

"What are you talking about over there?" A.J. asked. Tony leaned over to him and whispered something. Then A.J. started laughing. I simply shook my head at both of them.

"Okay, guys," Danny announced. "We're gonna go ahead and get started. First of all, thank you for participating in this project. I'm looking forward to this and having some fun in the magazine. I believe I've got everyone scheduled for their interviews except Chris. Chris, I need you to send me your info, and we'll get that set up. Everyone make sure you log in to the Yahoo site with the league username and password. Draft order's already set up, so let's have fun. By the way, menus are on the back table and the waitresses will be coming by to get your orders if you want anything. Also, bathrooms are at the back of the main bar. Any other questions?"

"Yeah. I got one." The voice came from a woman sitting at the end of the table. She wore a Red Sox cap tilted slightly to the side and a dark ponytail sticking out the back.

"Sure, Lisa. Go ahead."

"I just want to know which one of these butthead guys plan on finishing last." That caused a slight ruckus amongst the table.

"What makes you think one of the guys will finish last?" I responded. "It might be one of the ladies." There wasn't that much of a response after I said that. "It might even be you."

That got a rise out of everyone. She shot me a look of surprise at what I said but then responded, "Typical male. You think you know everything about sports."

"I don't know everything. But when I'm right, I do know how to serve it with a side of crow."

That brought a round of applause and a collective "oooh" from the guys at the table. Some of the women laughed, but the one who spoke up shot another glare at me. Then she lightened up, shook her head, and looked back at her laptop.

"Dude," A.J. said as he leaned over to me. "What was that?"

"Just some trash talk," I replied.

"Yeah. But from you?"

"It's no big deal."

"No big deal, my ass," Tony said quietly. "You did something right because she's still looking over here."

"Yeah, right," I said as I logged in.

"Chris, look up."

"What?"

"Just look up."

I looked over my laptop screen, and I saw she was look-ing at my direction with a smile on her face. When she saw I was looking at her, she quickly turned her glance back to her laptop but still smiling.

"Look at you, man," Tony said. "She is feeling you. You know what? That porn star brought the tiger out of you."

"What?"

"You wouldn't have snapped back the way you did, not even last week."

"He's right," A.J. added. "You would not have done that before. I think Tony's right

about you."

"And what's that?"

"Like rain..."

"Stop it. Not you, too."

Then twelve computers all chimed a baseball-themed song, signaling the start of the draft.

"Looks like we're ready to go," Danny said. "Good luck."

{ 10 }

On Monday morning, I tried to put the events of the weekend behind me. From being with Laura, meeting Lydia, and
the fantasy baseball banter, there was plenty to process. But
the one thing that kept popping up was what Tony told me.

Women are about to fall on your head like rain.

I was making my way to my work area when I peered
over to my right and saw Jennifer, one of my team members,
walking behind me.

"Good morning," I said as I let her catch up with me.
"Have a good weekend?"

"Yes," she said. "Very quiet. I did some gardening and
that was it. How about you?"

"Eventful."

"Oh really. How so?"

"My friend got engaged this weekend so we went out to
celebrate. Then I got invited at the last minute to a fantasy
baseball league sponsored by this local magazine and..."

"*River City Magazine?*" she interrupted.

"Yeah," I answered cautiously. "Why?"

"I read the article about it last month. Chris, you're going to be a local celebrity!"

"Oh, geez. That's the last thing I need."

"Chris, it'll be so awesome."

We got to our work area to join the rest of the team. April and Renee were having a conversation in the walkway while James was returning to his cubicle with a cup of coffee in his hand.

"Good morning," I said.

"Good morning to you," April replied. "Have a good weekend?"

"He's going to be in *River City Magazine!*" Jennifer responded.

"Really?" Renee asked. "What for?"

"There's a story about fantasy baseball," I tried to explain. "They got a league going and interviewing the participants."

"Well, well. We have ourselves a local celebrity."

"Look. It's no big deal."

"No big deal?" Jennifer chimed in. "All kinds of people are going to be reading about you."

"All kinds of women, too," April added.

"Oh goodness," I sighed. "You guys are too much."

"You know we're just trying to help," Renee kidded.

"Trust me, I know." Then I waved to everybody and said, "Well, I need to check in."

As I got to my work station, I heard footsteps coming in my direction. I turned around and saw May hurriedly rushing toward me, dropping her stuff off at her cubicle along the way.

"Good morning," I said. "You're in quite a rush."

"Good morning," she replied, slightly out of breath. "I wanted to catch you before the day started."

"Sure," I replied as I took my seat. "What's up?"

"Do you belong to a gym?"

"No, but I thought about checking out Richmond Fitness..."

"Great!" she replied with excitement. She handed me a voucher and said, "Why don't you check it out tonight."

"Tonight?"

"Yes, tonight. It's the last day of their March Madness promotion. If you sign up, you'll get a discount on your first three months, and I get a free month when you mention my name."

"But May..."

"I know, I know. I have procrastinated so badly on this. But I really hope you can go."

I took a long look at the voucher and finally said, "Okay. I'll swing out there and see what it looks like."

"Beautiful," she replied as she clapped her hands in approval. "Make sure you mention my name."

"I'll do that."

May left my area as I logged into my computer. As I was going through my calendar to go over my meeting schedule, I heard a knock on my cubicle opening. I turned around and saw James standing there.

"What's up?" I said.

"Not much," he replied. "The others had you all tied up about the magazine that I didn't even get a chance to say good morning."

"Well, good morning."

Looking at the voucher sitting on my desk, he said, "So May wants you to go to Richmond Fitness?"

"Yeah," I responded as I leaned back in my chair. "I thought about looking at that place anyway..."

"Do it!" he quickly blurted out. "Trust me."

"Hold up," I replied as I sat up. "Why'd you say it like that?"

"Let's just say there's plenty of motivation over there," he said softly with a sly smile.

"Motivation?"

"Oh yeah. Most of the women..." He then nodded his head in approval.

"What in the world? I thought you're supposed to be there to work out."

"I do work out," he assured me. "Look, this is all I'm saying. "There's some good looking women in there. Everybody's cool with each other. The staff is friendly, and it's a nice environment. If I can have a good time in there, I know you will. Just go, sign up, and start working out."

I took another look at May's voucher and said, "Okay. I'll take a look at it tonight."

"Good morning, Chris." The sound of Shelley's voice broke up the conversation James and I were having. He nodded to me and walked back to his cubicle as she peered into my area. "How are you this fine morning?"

"I'm well," I answered. "How are you and what event are you trying to recruit me for?"

"Now, Chris. You know I don't always come over here asking for things. But..." She slipped inside my cubicle and leaned against the partition. "I do need your help."

"Let me guess. Another job fair? Or is it a trade show this time?"

"Chris, why are you being difficult?" she huffed as she stomped her foot.

"I'm not being difficult. I just know what you're going to ask."

"Look, I need someone to help out with the trade show at the Raceway Pavilion this afternoon. Judy called in this morning with a family emergency, and I need another body at the table.

"Well," I said as I stared at May's voucher sitting on my desk. "Count me out. I've got another engagement. Maybe next time."

"Chris, I'm going to hold you to that," she replied. "I'll get you sooner or later." She left to go on her way, and I returned back to my computer, laughing to myself about the encounter.

{ 11 }

I arrived at Richmond Fitness that evening, not knowing
what to expect. May and James seemed to enjoy being members here, but the skeptic in me still had doubts. But as I
walked in, I saw exactly what James was talking about. Two
gorgeous women in workout gear walked past me on their
way out. They paused their conversation and politely said
hello. I waved back and smiled as I continued to the front
desk. It had a wooden floor covering the sections, and the
counter has the company logo welded onto the front. On top
was a marble counter with three computer screens and scan-
ners sitting at the desk partition. There was a female attendant dressed in a purple polo shirt and black pants with the
logo attached at the bottom of each sleeve. There was also
a man dressed in a blue dress shirt and tie along with grey
slacks.

"Good evening," he said. "How can I help you?"

"Well," I said. "I have this voucher for March Madness..."

"Great!" he responded. "I can take that." He took my
voucher and made his way around the desk to where I was
standing. He shook my hand and said, "My name is Darrell.
Glad to have you here. Why don't you come with me, and I'll
give you a tour of our facility."

We started our way toward the main floor. There were rows of elliptical machines, treadmills, and stationary bikes lined up to the right of me. I looked ahead and saw on the other side of the glass a swimming pool and a hot tub. Then I looked to my right and saw the three racquetball courts. Darrell led me to the center of the action and started to point out the exercise areas.

"What are you doing here?" I heard a female voice call out. Then a woman came over to us, dressed in a white T-shirt, black workout shorts, and tennis shoes. She stood there with a wide smile and her arms crossed in front. After taking a moment to look her over, I finally realized who she was.

"I remember you," I said with a smile. "You were at the fantasy baseball draft last night."

"You got it," she replied.

"You look a little different without that Red Sox cap on."

"Red Sox?" Darrell joked. "I'm so sorry."

"What?" she fired back. "And your team is…"

"Yankee blue all the way," he boasted.

"Oh God," she groaned. "Another Yankee to deal with."

"So," I butted in. "I never did catch your name."

"Lisa," she said quickly as she reached out her hand. "Lisa Robbins."

"Chris Wheeler," I replied as I shook her hand. "Nice to meet the last place finisher."

"Ha! Whatever, man," she responded as she pulled her hand away. "Oh, it's going to be so much fun winning this." Then she turned to Darrell and asked, "So is he signing up?"

"I'm working on it," he replied.

"You better," she said as she lightly punched my arm. "I need to keep an eye on my competition."

"I see," I replied. "Maybe I need to do the same thing."

"Yeah, right. Look, I gotta get back to it. See you soon."

Darrell and I both nodded as Lisa walked upstairs. We then walked into the men's locker room to continue with the tour.

"So what's up with you and her?" he asked.

"This thing for *River City Magazine*. They're doing a story on fantasy baseball, so they got a league going. We're in it."

"Oh, okay. So some smack talk going on?"

"You could say that."

"Looks like she loved it," he replied as he showed me the sauna.

"Come on. Are you serious?"

"She fired her shot. You took it, and dished it right back. She's going to be thinking about that for a while."

We exited the locker room and headed upstairs to the weight area. I saw people milling about and working out all over the place. Then I saw Lisa working out on the leg press. I caught her attention, and she nodded at me before starting her next set.

"You wanna stop the tour?" Darrell asked in a joking manner.

"What are you talking about?"

"So you can talk to your girl over there?"

"What? Nah, I'm good."

"Hey, Darrell," a woman said as she walked over to us. Her workout attire of a black top and lime green pants showed off her curves, and I found myself taking a glance of admiration. I looked up at her face to see her soft grey eyes to go along with her tanned skin and brown shoulder-length hair.

"Hey, Michelle," he responded. "How's the class going?"

"Good. Still would like to have some more people in there. Hint, hint."

"You still after me on that?"

"Damn right." Then she looked at me and said, "And you, too."

"Chris," Darrell said. "This is Michelle. She teaches kickboxing in Studio A. Michelle, this is Chris and..."

"Sign him up," she interrupted. Then she placed her hand gently on my arm, leaned in, and said, "Then you can take my class."

"Kickboxing?"

"It's a hell of a workout. And don't worry, nobody's there for an MMA tryout or anything. We're all having a good time."

"I guess I'll have to look into that," I replied.

"You do that." She looked back at Darrell and playfully pointed at him. "I'll deal with you later."

"Okay, Michelle. I still got a tour to do. You have fun with your workout."

"Thanks. Take care."

"Nice meeting you, Michelle," I called out as she walked away.

She waved and went back to her workout. I watched her for a few moments before turning my attention back to Darrell. He pointed me to the track area on the perimeter. As we took a short walk around, I looked inside to catch a brief glimpse of Lisa and Michelle. Soon, I was barely hearing anything Darrell had to say.

In fact, I didn't care too much about the tour anymore.

I was ready to sign up.

{ 12 }

The work week went by without a hitch, and I went home
wondering what the weekend had in store. I hadn't heard
from A.J. or Tony, but I wasn't all that worried because I
wasn't in the mood to be in the clubs anyway. As I was heat-
ing up dinner, I opened my laptop and glanced at my e-mails.
One of them was from the bookstore advertising a Friday
night jazz concert. Seeing that, I decided that would be my
plans for the night.

After dinner, I headed out to the bookstore. When I got
there, the parking lot was just about full. I happened to find
one parking space in the back of the lot, and I went inside. I
could hear the soft sounds of a jazz standard playing in the
background. Then a sultry female voice began to sing over
the music, and it immediately drew my attention over to the
café area where quite a crowd had assembled. But then I felt
someone tapping my arm. I turned around and saw Lydia
standing behind me.

"Hey, stranger," she said. "You made it. And to think, I
was about to send you an e-mail to get you out here."

"Well, I made it," I replied.

"How do like the band?" she asked as she looked out to
the café.

"Sounds good. Who is it?"

"Miss Elle and the Jazz Gents. This was a hard get because they're really popular in town." Then she turned to me and asked, "So how have you been?"

"Doing good. Nothing crazy's happening, so I can't complain. How are things here?"

The song ended and there was a courteous applause for the performance. Then Lydia replied, "Good. We've got a lot of stuff booked. By the way, Stacie says hello."

As the music played again, the singer made her way through the café toward Lydia and I. As she sauntered over, I took note of the amount of red all about her. Her red hair, her red lipstick, her red blouse, and her bright red heels stood out. The only thing non-red on her was her black knee-length skirt and pantyhose. She smiled as she walked to us as she gently brushed some hair off the left side of her face.

"How are we sounding?" she asked Lydia.

"Everything sounds good," she responded. "The crowd is definitely enjoying themselves."

"Good. Good." Then Elle turned to me and asked, "How about you?"

"I'm enjoying it."

"Elle," Lydia cut in. "This is my friend Chris Wheeler."

"Nice to meet you, Elle," I said as I reached out my hand.

"Likewise," she replied. She held my hand for a moment as she quizzically studied my face. "Your name sounds familiar. Do you happen to know Valerie Taylor?"

"I do. We've spent some time together."

"That's what I thought. She's a friend of mine, and she brought up your name a few times."

"I hope she had good things to say."

"Oh, absolutely," she replied. "She thought the world of you." She then took her other hands and clasped it on top of our handshake. "I can definitely see why." She looked back toward the band and then back to me. "I'm going to get back to the guys. You gonna stay around?"

"Sure. I'll be here."

"Good. Enjoy the show." She let go of my hand and gently patted me on the forearm. Then she gave me a wink and a smile as she made her way around the room and back to her bandmates. As I watched, I could feel someone tugging on my arm. I looked down and saw Lydia staring at me with a curious smile on her face.

"What?" I asked.

"What was that?"

"Nothing."

"Yeah, right. Did you see the way she looked at you?"

"The way she looked at me? What are you talking about?"

"Come on, Chris," she said. Then she playfully poked me in the arm. "You know what? You're dangerous."

"Dangerous?" I replied before I started laughing.

"Yes. You are dangerous," she responded while taking a step away from me.

"Come on, Lydia."

"No, no, no. I need to keep my distance." She then checked her watch. "Look, I need to go to the back office and take care of a couple of things. I'll catch up with you later."

"Okay. See you later."

Lydia left the café area, leaving me to kick back and listen to Elle and her band

{ 13 }

I stayed until closing time. Then music was good, and Elle could really sing. The café stayed crowded through the entire performance, and the rest of the bookstore had plenty of people milling about. After the show, the crowd quickly filed out of the establishment. Soon the only people in the café were Elle and the band, Lydia, and me. As I watched the band pack up their stuff, Lydia slid next to me with quite a large smile on her face.

"You stayed the whole time," she said as she tapped me on the small of my back.

"It was a good show," I replied. "Elle and her band played some good jazz."

"I know. We had a good crowd, too."

"Hey guys," Elle said as she and her group approached us. "We're getting ready to get out of here. Lydia, this was a good venue."

"Thanks a bunch. You guys were great."

"Thanks. I'm glad you enjoyed it. What about you, Chris?"

"Good show," I answered. "You're a wonderful singer."

"Thank you so much." Then she reached into her purse and pulled out a business card. She handed it to me and said,

"Our website info is on the card. Sign up for the newsletter and see where we're playing next."

"Sounds like an invitation," I replied.

"You could call it that," she responded with a soft smile.

"Well," I said as I reached out to shake her hand. "I look forward to seeing you again."

She shook my hand, and we held that pose for a moment. Then she left go and leaned forward to me. I went to meet her halfway when she planted a slow, soft kiss on my cheek as she wrapped her arm around my neck and hugged me.

"See you soon," she said as she let go of me.

"Likewise," I replied.

She and her bandmates passed by Lydia and me and headed to the front exit. As they headed out, I spotted Lydia giving me a strange look.

"Okay. What was that?" she inquired.

"What was what?" I answered. "We just said goodbye."

"Goodbye, huh? That was not just goodbye, buddy."

'Geez. Will you stop it?"

"Hey, Lydia," a male voice called out. We looked up and saw the employee standing at the front door. "I'm about to lock up."

"Hold on. Let me get my stuff and head out."

"I'll wait up for you," I said.

She ran off to the back of the store as I made my way to the front door.

"Fun night, huh?" the guy asked.

"It was," I replied. "Lydia's picking up right where Stacie left off."

"That's what I heard. I've been working here about a month, and it seems like something's always going on around here."

"Okay, guys," Lydia said as she approached the door with two bags slung over her shoulder. "I'm ready."

The guy opened the door to let us out. Lydia pointed to her blue Honda parked in the rear. I was parked about three spots from her so I walked with her to our cars.

"That was a fun night," she said. "I'm glad you came out."

"Me, too," I replied. "Better than sitting at home."

"Well, you better not be sitting at home too many times. I want to see you at more events, mister."

"I will, I will. But you know..."

"You're a busy guy?" she cut with a laugh as we arrived at her car. "I'm fully aware of that."

She unlocked her car and opened the back door. Then she put her bags in the back seat before turning back to me. I watched her nervously bite her lower lip as she rocked back and forth on her heels.

"What's on your mind?" I asked.

"I was thinking...well..." Then she started laughing.

"What?" I pressed on.

"I was just wondering if you were going to say goodbye to me the same way you did Elle?" she blurted out.

"You mean...geez. That was nothing." Then I opened up my arms and said, "Come here."

She moved over to me and wrapped her arms tightly around my waist. "You're still dangerous."

"No, I'm not."

"Yes, you are. I bet you treated Stacie the same as you did Elle."

"Stacie and I are friends."

"I know what you're saying," she said as she let go of me. "But I bet if she had been here longer, she would've been in your bed."

"Oh come on!" I replied. Then I laughed out at her remark. "You know what? I'm going home on that." I started to walk to my car but then I turned around and said, "Unless..."

"No!" she snapped back. "I'm going home. You have a good night." She got in her car and turned on the ignition. As she pulled out of her parking space, she waved goodbye with a wide smile on her face.

{ 14 }

The next morning, I packed my gym bag and made my way to Richmond Fitness. I parked my car near the back of the parking lot. The lot was quite occupied, and I could tell a lot of people had the same intentions of getting in a morning workout. After getting inside and changing in the locker room, I made my way to one of the stationary bikes. I put on my headphones to my music player and started pedaling.

After a few minutes, I got lost in my music and the rhythm of my legs rotating through each revolution. I looked up for a moment to notice five others on the same line of bikes, each with their headphones on and locked into their own rhythm. When I turned back to look at the console, I saw a woman standing directly over it. She was wearing a black T-shirt and red workout tights. Her wide smile indicated to me that we've met before.

"Hey there," she said as I took my headphones off. "Remember me?"

"Um," I tried to answer. "Not really."

"March Madness? Darrell gave you a tour of the place?"

"Darrell…Darrell. Okay, I remember Darrell."

"Kickboxing?"

"Kickboxing...kick...oh, Michelle. Okay, now I remember. Hey there."

She leaned back and laughed. "Hey yourself. I see he did a good job. He got you signed up."

"Yeah. I liked what I saw, so I put my signature down."

"That's awesome. So what are you working on this morning?"

"Working on?" I responded, unsure of what she was referring to.

"Yeah. Chest? Legs? Back?"

"I don't know," I replied as I leaned forward to grab my water bottle to take a sip. "It's been a while so...maybe a leg press or two."

"Well, that's a start. But make sure you take it easy, champ. Don't get all crazy the first time out."

"I'll try not to. So what about you?"

"Just cardio today. But hey, don't forget Tuesday and Thursday at seven."

"What about...oh, your class. You're going to stay on me for that, aren't you?"

"You damn right I am." She then made her way past me toward the treadmills. But as she walked by, she dragged her hand across my arm to my shoulder where she squeezed it firmly a couple of times. "Have a good workout."

As she walked away, I turned around as far as I could while keeping my pace on the bike. I couldn't help but notice her shape move in a perfect harmony as she strode away. I turned back to my exercise, whistling to myself and shaking my head as I put my headphones back on.

After about forty-five minutes of riding, I made my way upstairs to the weights area. With so many machines around, I wasn't quite sure where to start. I finally decided to follow along with what I told Michelle and walked over to the leg press machines. The lack of activity in my body became increasingly evident as I had to lighten the weight load after each set. After leg presses, calf raises, and leg curls, my muscles were tight and sore.

To loosen up, I stretched out a bit and made my way to the track area that looped around the outside edge of the floor. As I started, a couple of runners jogged past me, and I quickly decided that running was not in the cards this morning. So I walked along the inside lane and started to put my music together and my headphones on.

"Hey!" I heard someone call out. I happened to look down at the basketball courts below. There was one game going on to the left and a couple of people shooting at the main hoop on the right. Then I picked up on who was calling me. Lisa was standing at the free throw line with a basketball pinned at her hip with a wide grin on her face.

"Hey, yourself!" I called back.

"How many?" she replied, circling her finger in the air.

I shrugged my shoulders at her response.

"Well, give me ten!"

"Ten what?"

"Ten laps, man."

"You're crazy. I'm not running ten laps."

"Then walk 'em." She clapped her hands and pointed in the direction I was going, laughing the whole time. "Let's go!" I gave her a look of astonishment at what she was asking but her finger remained pointed outward.

So I shook my head, put my headphones on, and start walking. With the music in my ears, I was able to get a decent pace going to the point that I lost count of how many times I went around. But then I happened to glance down at the courts. Lisa was playing in one of the two games and as she was heading back down the court on defense, she looked up at me and held up three fingers.

"She's counting my laps?" I muttered to myself. I shook it off and kept up my pace, determined to get this challenge finished. But every time I would pass by and steal a glance down, I could see she was still keeping tabs on me.

When I completed my final lap, I looked down at the court and saw that Lisa was nowhere to be found. I felt disgruntled for getting put through this exercise and having the instigator take off. But when I got to the edge of the next partition, I found her leaning against the wall with a big smile on her face. She offered me a fist bump as I peeled off the track.

"Good job," she said. "Next time you'll run 'em, right?"

"Shit no," I replied. "I did enough running in high school."

"Oh really. What sport?"

"Baseball." As we made our downstairs, I continued. "Our coach was also assistant coach for the football team, and he ran our asses like crazy. Sometimes I felt like we were getting ready for fall camp instead of a game."

"That sounds like it stunk. Were you guys any good?"

"If you call a forty-game losing streak any good," I joked.

"Ouch. I think the longest I ever went through was four games in college."

As we got to the first floor, Lisa motioned over to the café area by the front door. The lone person there was the male attendant standing by the counter.

"What's up, guys?" he said. "What can I get for you?"

"Two Gatorades," she replied.

"You got it." He went back to the refrigerator and pulled out two bottles. "Put this on your account?"

"Sure." She pulled out her keys from her pocket and held out her scan card from the key chain. The attendant scanned it and approved the sale. Then Lisa handed one of the bottles to me.

"Thanks," I replied, surprised at her gesture.

"No problem. It's the least I could do since you did knock out those laps for me."

We both had a good laugh as we took our seats at the raised table sitting at the front window. Lisa opened her bottle and took a long swig. I was about to open my bottle, but instead I sat back and watched her take her drink and then smile at me.

"So a four game losing streak in college?" I asked. "Where did you play?"

"University of New Haven. Division Two."

"You start?"

"Three years. Sixteen points, eight assists senior year. In fact, you're looking at number three all-time in assists."

"Look out," I replied as I cracked open my bottle. I took a sip and asked, "But I thought you were a baseball person? With the Red Sox cap at all?"

She took another drink from her bottle and started laughing. "I'm from Massachusetts. Boston teams are in my DNA."

"Wait a minute," I replied. "Massachusetts and Connecticut. How in the hell did you end up in Richmond?"

"Work. My office moved down here as part of a merger."

"Oh, you must work for Middletown Financial. I read about that move in the paper."

"You got it." Lisa took a glance at the TV screen and sighed. "Crap. I gotta get out of here. I promised Danny I'd do my interview with her this afternoon to get it out of the way." She got out of her seat and said, "Good catching up with you."

"You too," I replied. "How about next time we see each other there are no laps involved?"

"You're funny," she said. "I'd love to get together with you. Let me give you my number." As I typed her digits into my phone, she leaned in and whispered, "You better use it."

"Oh, I will," I replied. Then I sent her a quick text. "Now you've got my number." I looked up at her and said, "And you better use it."

"Listen to you!" she cracked back as she slapped me on the shoulder. "Wise guy. I gotta run. Don't be a stranger." She then headed toward the exit.

I made my way to the locker room to change. After changing and packing up, I headed to the exit.

"Hey!" I heard someone call out. I turned around and saw Michelle standing by the counter.

"Have a good one," she said with a smile. "And take my class!"

{ 15 }

*Season starts Monday. You and I play first. Ready to get
your ass kicked lol?*

My morning began with Lisa's trash talk of a text about
the upcoming season. I leaned back in my cubicle and
laughed at what she said. So I responded,

*It's a long season, lady. Too bad you're starting in last place
lol.*

"What are you laughing at?" I heard Jennifer ask me. I
looked up and saw her staring me from my cubicle opening.
"Someone special I hope?"

"Oh, stop it," I replied. "It's not even like that."

"You sure?"

"Yes." I turned to face her and said, "If you must know,
it's fantasy baseball season and someone in my magazine
league just texted me a reminder that we've facing off this
week."

Jennifer slipped inside my cubicle and leaned against my
desk. "So what's her name?"

"What makes you think it's a woman?"

"Because men don't normally send other men texts like that." She leaned in closer and whispered, "I know it's a woman, and I know she likes you."

"Oh boy," I hesitated. She leaned back and folded her arms, letting me know she wasn't leaving until I dished out a name. "Okay. Her name is Lisa."

"I knew it," she quietly celebrated as she gave slight fist pump. "So tell me about her."

"No," I replied. "I've already told you too much."

"Come on, Chris."

"No. I'm not saying a thing. Besides..."

"What's so funny?" I heard male voice call out. I looked up and saw Mr. Drake standing at my cubicle opening.

"Oh. Mr. Drake...hi," I said. "Jennifer and I were just talking about a text I got, that's all."

"No problem at all. I didn't mean to catch you by surprise."

"Chris, I'll leave you alone for now," she said. She started out of my cubicle but then turned around and said, "But you know..."

"I know, I know. You'll want details later."

Jennifer laughed and pointed her finger at me. "Get after it, guy." She walked off as I just shook my head.

"What can I do for you, sir?" I asked as I turned my attention back to Mr. Drake.

"Nothing major. Just had a question for you."

"Sure."

"You like jazz?"

"Yeah."

"Good. Here." He handed me two tickets. "This is for the museum Saturday night."

"I thought the museum was free," I replied as I took the tickers from him.

"It is, but this is a bit different. Big event's going on after hours, and you have to have a ticket to get in. It's supposed to be a really good jazz concert, but the wife and I can't make it."

"That's too bad."

"No, that's not the case. My wife's cousin's son just got engaged. There's going to be a big party for them at her cousin's place in Maryland."

"Wow," I said as I leaned back in my seat. "Making the big leap, huh?"

"I've met her, Chris. He's got a good one. Maybe one of these days..."

"I know. I hear it from everybody around here. I'll keep you posted when it happens."

"I'll hold you to that," he replied with a slight laugh. "Well, enjoy the concert."

"I will. Thanks, Mr. Drake."

"No problem. Have a good one." He left my cubicle and I turned around to face my computer. Then my cell phone rang.

"Hello," I answered.

"Chris, it's Danny from the magazine. How are you?"

"I'm doing fine. What's up?"

"Season's starting on Monday, and I need to get your interview done. Can you meet me Friday for lunch?"

"That should be fine," I replied as I checked my calendar on my computer. "Where do you want to meet?"

"Scott's Bistro over by the Boulevard work?"

"Sure. Sounds like you're trying to get out of the office."

"It's crazy around here. Along with our deadlines, out annual bridal issue is due out. It's supposed to be a really nice day, and I wouldn't mind being outside for a bit."

"Okay. So I'll see you then."

"Sounds good. Take care."

I hung up my call, put my phone back in my pocket, and focused back on my work. Just as I settled in, my cell phone buzzed again. I took it back out of my pocket and saw I got another text message. This one was from Laura.

Hey babe. I was up early and I was thinking about you. There's an Erotic Expo in Richmond in a couple of months, and I may be back in town for that. I'll let you know how things work out. If I can make it, I'd love to see you and have some time for Round Two lol. Kisses!!

"Wow," I said quietly to myself. "Laura."

As I tried to focus and get back to work, my cell phone buzzed again. I recognized the area code as coming from Northern Virginia but I didn't know who it was.

"Hello," I answered.

"Chris, it's Gerald."

"Hey! What going on with you?"

"Not much. I figured I'd grab you before school started. What are you doing tonight?"

"Nothing. What's going on?"

"I'm coming down to Richmond."

"Tonight? Aren't you in the middle of the season?"

"Yeah, but I'm giving the kids the day off. We've had to play a bunch of makeup games the past couple of weeks because of rainouts. They could use some rest before the postseason."

"So what's going on in Richmond?"

"Norfolk State's in town to play VCU. One of my former players pitches for Norfolk State. He texted me last night that they're giving him the start. So I'm coming down to watch him."

"That's awesome, man. Yeah, I'll meet you at the Diamond. Seven o'clock game, right?"

"Yeah."

"Cool. See you tonight then."

"Okay. Peace."

I hung up my call with Gerald and turned back to my computer, finally getting back to my work schedule.

{ 16 }

After work, I went home and changed into some casual gear. I grabbed a quick dinner and then headed out to the Diamond. Traffic was relatively light, and it didn't take me long to get to the stadium. I parked near the front entrance, paid my way in, and went up the steps to the seating areas. I immediately spotted Gerald wearing his John Adams baseball cap sitting about five rows down from the bottom.

"What's going on, man?" I called out as I approached his row. "You're representing even away from home?"

"Hey man," he replied. "Gotta do it."

I stepped across a couple and made my way to sit next to him. We exchanged a head nod and a fist bump before I sat down. "So Norfolk State's starting pitcher is one of your guys?"

"Manny Morris," he said, pointing out to the visiting bullpen where I saw a tall, lanky kid warming up. "First college signee of my program."

"Congrats, man."

"Best advertisement I could ask for. Tryout numbers jumped the next season after the kids saw Manny sign his letter of intent."

"I bet. So what does he have?"

"Two-seam, four-seam, and a change. He told me he's been working on a curve, so I'm curious to see it."

"Hope he's not too good," a lady in front of us said as she turned to face us. She was wearing a black VCU T-shirt and jeans along with her open-toed sandals. As she looked at us, I found myself staring at my reflection in her sunglasses.

"Oh, that's right," I responded. "UVA cleaned your clocks the other night."

"It was not pretty. Anyway, good luck to you guys."

"Thanks," Gerald replied. Then he turned to me and asked, "So what's going on with you?"

"Things are good."

"But what's really going on?"

"Oh that," I replied. "Well, interesting stuff."

"Interesting? How?"

I leaned in and said, "One on my boys from college tried out this mental trick on me. He told me to write down something about being a nice guy and then rip it up. That's supposed to clear the path for women to come flocking."

"Is it working?"

"Well, that night I ran into someone I knew from high school."

"So what..." He caught himself, realizing where I was heading with the story. Then he started laughing. "Never mind."

Just then the public address announcer asked for the crowd to stand for the National Anthem. Gerald and I stopped our conversation and stood with everyone else. When the last note was played, there was a round of applause before everyone took their seats.

When we sat down, I tapped him on the arm and motioned for him to come closer. Then I whispered, "Now I got two chicks at my gym checking me out. One of them texted me today."

"Go ahead now. Sounds like your friend's idea may be working."

"So what's happening at Adams?" I asked as we watched the first Norfolk State batter approach the plate.

"Brenda Franklin just got married."

"To who?"

"Somebody you know."

"Who?"

"Derek Rivers."

"Derek!" I exclaimed. "Get the...Derek?"

"Yeah."

"That Poindexter?"

"What's the deal? Your Dad thinks he's a decent guy."

"Derek Rivers got messed with like crazy at Adams and especially by the Franklin sisters. Did you hear the story about Senior Prank Week?"

"Tampons hanging from his locker?" he replied as he leaned back. "I heard about that. But they both say all is for-given, that they were just kids."

"Bullshit," I heard from below. The woman who had talked to us before turned around to face us. "I don't mean to pry into your conversation but that sounds like someone was desperate to get married just to say they were married. They just needed to find a sucker."

"Sounds like you know a little something about that."

"Oh yeah. I was the sucker." She then took off her shades and I looked into her piercing grey eyes.

"Wait a minute," I said. "You look familiar."

"You too," she replied as she took another look at me. "You know what? Bailey's."

"Fantasy baseball draft."

"Yes!" she said with a grand smile. "Now I remember you. You're Chris, right?"

"Yeah," I answered curiously. "That's me. And you are…"

"Sheila," she replied as we shook hands. "Sheila Ross."

"Nice to meet you. So why did you call yourself a sucker?"

"Because when I was a sophomore in college, I fell in love with a senior. He graduated and came to VCU for grad school. He said he loved me and couldn't bear the thought of a long-distance relationship. So instead of staying at school in Michigan, guess what I did?"

"I see…and I bet it didn't end well," I said as I looked up to watch a Norfolk State batter walk up to the plate. The scoreboard showed there were two outs in the top of the first inning. I turned back to her and asked, "So how long…"

"Seven years of misery," she replied. "But in the end, I can't be too upset. I got three degrees from VCU, I'm closer than ever to my brother, and I get to hang out with that bundle of energy in black and gold over there."

I looked down the aisle and saw a young boy dressed in a gold shirt and black shorts chatting gleefully with three other boys his age.

"Nephew?" I asked.

"You got it. I told my brother I'd bring him to the game, so he and his wife can have a mid-week date night. Little guy happened to run into some friends from his Little League team, and they're having a ball.

Then a loud cheer erupted. We looked up and saw a hitter walking in dejection toward the Norfolk State dugout as the VCU team ran off the field. As Norfolk State took the field, I looked back at Gerald as he intently watched his former player take his warm-up pitches.

"You want to get back to the game with your friend?" she asked.

"Yeah, I better. But I would like..."

"Sure. I'd love to get together with you," she said with a wink and a smile. "Let me get you my business card." As she reached for her purse, I leaned back to join Gerald.

"Hey Manny!" he yelled. "Don't fall in love with your changeup!"

The lanky kid on the mound glanced into the stands. He picked up on Gerald's voice and his position in the stands, gave a slight smile, nodded his head, and got back to his warm-up.

"Chris, I saw that wink, you know," he whispered as he leaned over to me.

"What wink?" I replied.

"Don't play dumb, man. I saw the look on her face. You gonna get on that or what?"

"Come on, man."

"Hey," Sheila said as she poked me in the leg with her business card. "Give me a call."

"Thanks. I'll do that."

"Good." She then turned her attention to her nephew down the aisle. "J.J., where are you going?"

"Nowhere, Aunt Sheila," the boy called out.

"Okay. You and your friends stay right where you are so I can see you, understood?"

She waved back at me and turned her attention to the game and the children. I leaned back and looked at the card she gave me.

"A professor, huh?" Gerald observed.

"I thought you were paying attention to your guy."

"I am." The first batter made his way into the batter's box, took his stance, and waited for the pitcher to deliver. "Watch this. Leadoff guy's a lefty. Guarantee you Manny starts him two-seamer away." We watched his former player set himself, go into his motion, and deliver his pitch. The baseball smacked into the catcher's mitt and the umpire called out a strike. "Yep, same old Manny."

As Gerald and I watched the game, I took another look at Sheila's card. I turned it over and saw she had written a note on the back.

BTW...I'm free this weekend. XOXO

"I saw that, too," Gerald laughed.

{ 17 }

I almost didn't make it to my lunch meeting with Danny Friday. There was an emergency meeting called at work, and it ran way longer than it needed to. When it was finally over, it was well past eleven, and I didn't have much time to get into the city. I quickly got to my desk, checked my e-mails for any other surprises, and headed out.

I drove to the Boulevard and found a space on the street about a block from the bistro. When I got there, I saw Danny taking a seat at the outside patio. She was wearing a peach-colored blouse and a knee-length skirt along with her white high heels. She was engrossed in her iPhone as I approached.

"Hey there," I said as I took a seat. "I hope I wasn't late."

"No, you're fine," she replied as she looked up at me. We quickly shook hands as she put away her phone. "The e-mails just keep coming."

"Deadlines?"

"Deadlines, leads, openings…it never ends. But enough about that. How are you?"

"Okay. Emergency meeting to put out some fires, but otherwise, I'm not complaining."

"The season starts Monday. You ready?"

"Yeah," I replied as I leaned back in my chair. "I'm ready. I was reminded earlier this week."

"Hello," a waitress said as she came to our table. "My name is Alex, and I'll be your waitress today. Are you ready to order, or do you need a minute?"

"Give us a bit if you don't mind," I said as I picked up a menu at the side of the table stacked by the condiments. "But I would like some water."

"Me too," Danny added.

"Sure thing," the waitress said. "I'll be right back."

"So what exactly are we doing with this interview?" I asked as I scanned the menu.

"Basic stuff," Danny replied. "About who you are and how you got into fantasy sports." Then she put her menu down and looked directly at me. "But not right now."

"Not right now? What do you mean?"

"I've got something else I want to ask you."

"Okay," I replied as I put down my menu. "What's up?"

She leaned in and asked, "So what's up with you and Lisa?"

"Lisa? What about Lisa?"

"Didn't you get a reminder about the start of the season?"

"Yeah, I got a reminder. No big deal."

Danny stared at me with a sly smile on her face. "I know where that 'reminder' came from."

"Here are your waters, guys," the waitress said as she approached our table. She set down a glass in front of each of us. "Are you ready to order?"

"Sure," Danny responded. "Let me get the chicken panini and a side Caesar salad."

"I'll take the roast beef and some chips," I added.

"Okay. I'll be back with your orders." Then she left to go tend to another table.

"So what about Lisa?" Danny started again.

"What about her?"

"I heard a rumor you two met up at the gym and she watched you go around the track."

"What?" I responded. Fearing my answer was a bit loud, I took a look around to see if anyone heard me. There was only a group of four people nearby, and they didn't seem to notice my outburst. I returned my attention to Danny and took a deep breath. "How did you know that?"

"She told me."

"She told you?"

"Chris, she and I go back. We were teammates in high school and college. I know how she operates."

"Operates?"

She smiled at me and said, "When Lisa starts busting a guy's balls...well, let's just say that's her way of showing interest."

"Are you saying Lisa likes me?"

"She kind of hinted at that." Danny paused and then said, "She's not the only one who was checking you out."

"Not the only one?" I put my hands on top of my head and then ran them down the sides of my face as I took a deep breath. "Who else?"

"Tricia Welles mentioned you."

"Who's that?"

"She was the one in the Braves shirt sitting next to me."

"Oh," I said, trying to recall her. "I think I remember. But, man…" Then I mumbled, "I thought it was Sheila."

"Sheila?" Danny asked as she picked up on my words. "Dr. Ross? Oh, do tell."

"Danny?" I sighed and continued. "Okay, I ran into her at the VCU game last night."

She broke out in laughter and then said, "Chris, you're hot and you don't even know it."

I tilted my head back and stared at the sky in disbelief. I could hear Danny laughing in the background as I was trying to digest everything she was telling. I looked back at her and asked, "Anyone else I should know about?"

Danny paused before shaking her head no.

"You sure?" I inquired. "That pause…"

"Nothing," she replied.

"Okay guys," the waitress said. "Here are your orders. If you need anything else, let me know."

As she left, I saw Danny take out a small digital camera from her purse. She pointed it at my direction and said, "Smile."

"What's that for?" I asked.

"I need a picture for the article. Besides, we did come here to do your interview."

{ 18 }

After work, I headed home to grab my workout gear before heading to Richmond Fitness. As I pulled out of my driveway, my cell phone rang. I looked at the display saw Damon was on the other line. So I answered and put him on speaker.

"Hey!" I called out.

"What's up, man?"

"What the hell have you done to me?"

"What are you talking about?"

"Man, if you only knew…"

"It's working, isn't it?" he asked with a hint of laughter in his voice.

"Damon…"

"It's working. You ripped up the 'nice guy' paper, and now look at you. "You got women checking you out, right?"

"Well, yeah," I answered hesitantly.

"So what's the problem? Oh, that's right. You don't know how to handle all this attention."

"Come on, man."

As I pulled up to a stop light, I could hear the sound of sirens blaring in the distance. I looked up and saw there were two fire trucks at the previous light, heading in the other direction.

"Look, what are we talking about?" Damon asked. "Who are you talking to besides the porn star?"

"That's my classmate from high school!"

"Okay. Okay," he replied in a mocking tone. "It's you classmate from high school."

"Will you stop it?" I fired back at him.

"Fine," he replied. "Now who else?"

"There's a girl at the bookstore," I sighed, not liking where this interrogation was going. "She thinks…"

The light turned green, and I started along the intersection when a minivan sped up to get into the lane I was in. Then it slowed down in front of me, and I had to tap my brakes. I threw up my hands in frustration as it drove off along its way.

"She thinks what?" Damon asked.

"She thinks I'm dangerous."

"Dangerous? You know what? I like that. She's feeling you but doesn't want to get too close. Because you know…"

"Come on, man," I replied as I got back up to speed. "Is that all you think about? Fucking?"

"Of course not. But hey…"

"Can we be serious here?"

"Okay. Let's be serious. Who else are you talking to?"

"A couple of women at the gym, a jazz singer, and somebody I met at a baseball game last night."

"Go ahead with yourself," he praised me. "Looks like you're setting a nice table. Now it's time to eat."

"Eat?" I yelled. "This is not a buffet. We're talking about women here."

"I know we are. But follow me on this one."

"Okay," I relented. I turned into the parking lot of Richmond Fitness and parked around the middle of the lot. "Lay it on me."

"Let's say you're in line at the buffet. You start at the entrée section, and there's everything you can imagine. Chicken, turkey, fish, steak, you name it. But before you can say anything, they hand you a plate with a slice of meatloaf."

"Meatloaf?"

"Yep. Plain ass meatloaf."

"What in the world..."

"Just hold on. We're getting there. Now, let's keep going. You get to the vegetable section, and they got mashed potatoes and gravy, all kinds of greens, carrots, corn, everything. You hand over your plate and before you say anything...bam. They give you peas and hand back the plate."

"Peas? Damon?"

"Chris, you'll see where I'm going in a sec. So let's get to dessert. Cakes, pies, pudding, and some exotic shit that looks great. But instead, they hand you Jell-O."

"Jell-O?"

"Yes. Jell-O. And it's not even a flavor you like. So here's the meal. Do you know what some guys do? Sit down and eat without saying a word. They hope the next time they come to the buffet, they can get something different. But every time, the same thing happens. Finally, they resign to the fact this is all they can get. Then they start telling you how much they love meatloaf."

"Meatloaf, peas, and Jell-O? What the fuck, man?"

"You don't have to settle, dumbass!" he replied. "You know what you like. You know what turns your head. You know what turns you on. Go for it. The 'nice guy' in you settles for meatloaf. Fuck the meatloaf, fuck the peas, and fuck the damn Jell-O. You have the right to choose."

"Choose?"

"Yes! Fix your own plate."

That's when I heard a knock on my window. I looked up and Lisa staring at me. She smiled, waved, and then stuck her tongue out at me.

I rolled down my window and asked in a joking manner, "What are you doing?"

"Are you gonna work out or sit in your car all day?" she cracked back.

"I'll be in there. Just talking to my friend from college."

"Hi, friend from college!" she yelled into my phone.

"Hey, what's up?" Damon replied.

"Tell him to get his ass out of the car. It's time to work out."

"Give me a sec, and I'll do that."

"See you inside." she said to me.

"I'm coming."

Lisa waved and then ran off to the entrance. I rolled my window back up and returned to my call.

"Who was that?" Damon asked.

"Lisa," I answered. "She's in my fantasy baseball league."

"Well, don't let me hold you up. Go see your girl."

"I will."

"Fix your plate, Chris."

{ 19 }

After I got changed, I headed toward the treadmills. But before I got situated, I heard someone call out, "Hey!" I looked back and saw Lisa waving at me.

"What's up?" I asked as I stepped away from the machine.

"What are you working on?"

"I don't know. Maybe upper body."

"Work out with me tonight."

"Work out with you tonight?" I replied. "What's going on?"

"Nothing." Then she pointed to the cycling studio. "I was thinking about trying that, but I don't want to go by myself."

"So you want another guinea pig to go along with you?" I joked. "Or is there something else?"

"Like what?"

"Well, a little birdie told me you like to bust a guy's balls when you get the chance."

She broke out in laughter at my sentence. Then she said, "You talked to Danny, didn't you? What did she tell you?"

"Nothing," I responded with a smile.

"Bullshit," she replied as she punched me in the arm. "What did she say?"

"Oh no. A workout and information? That's gonna cost you."

"Oh man, Chris. Okay, recovery shake at the café is on me. Deal?"

"I guess that'll be enough," I said. "For now."

Lisa shook her head at me as we walked over to the studio. "Now what did she say?"

"She said you like to get after a guy if you really like him."

"I do not!" Her face was open with feigned shock as I told her what Danny had said. I started laughing when I saw her expression.

"Then why would she say that?"

"She's talking about Kelvin. He was this guy I met junior year. I really liked him, but I didn't know how to tell him."

"So you started pushing his buttons?" I asked as we entered the studio.

"You could say that."

"So what happened?"

"Let's just say he wasn't feeling it," she sighed.

"Hey girl!" a voice called out. I saw a woman walk over to us with a wide smile and an upward hand waiting for a high five. "You finally came in."

"Yeah, I'm here," she replied as she gave her a high five. "I'm going for it."

"Glad you could make it. You're gonna have fun." Then she looked over at me. "I see you brought someone else along."

"Couldn't do it alone tonight. Valerie, this is Chris."

"Hey Chris!" she said as she gave me a spirited high five. "Glad you came, too."

"Thanks. What am I in for?"

"Don't worry. You are going to have so much fun. Just get situated, and we'll get started soon, okay? Good to have you." She went over to talk to a couple of other people in the studio as Lisa and I claimed a couple of bikes near the back of the room.

"She's always that enthusiastic?" I asked as I adjusted my seat.

"Wait until we get started," she replied. "She'll ramp it up to eleven."

"So you've taken her class before?"

"It was a thirty minute class a while back. She's been after me to take another one of her classes. So I'm in here now.

"So this is another thirty?" I asked as I started to pedal.

"Oh no," she said as she hopped onto her seat. "This is a sixty minute class."

"Wha...What?" I replied as I looked at her in shock. "Sixty minutes? On this bike?" Lisa started laughing at my questions. "Holy shit. Danny was right."

"Right about what?"

"You do like to bust a guy's balls."

Lisa laughed ever louder at that statement as she made an adjustment to her bike. "I could tell some stories about her, too."

"Okay, everyone!" Valerie shouted through her microphone perched on her ear. "Who's ready for a great workout?" There were rousing cheers throughout the studio. I looked at Lisa, and she gave me a thumbs-up. I shook my head and dropped it into my chest, trying to psyche myself up for this exercise.

Over the course of sixty minutes, I found out just how out of shape I was. My legs were aching around the twenty minute mark, and the climbs and chases made them hurt even more. Sweat was pouring from my face, and I could feel my shirt sticking to my back. From time to time I looked over at Lisa and saw her pedaling away, focused solely on Valerie's instructions.

After the session was done, and we went through some post-ride stretching, Valerie yelled, "We are done! Yay! You made it! Give yourself a hand!" There were cheers and applause all around. I couldn't muster up enough energy to do either. Instead I slowly made my way to the paper towels and sanitizer located near the door. As I took out a couple of sheets, Valerie came over with a wide smile and open hand waiting for a high five. I weakly gave her hand a slap.

"Good job!" she said. "You made it all the way through."

"If you call it that," I replied.

"Hey, it'll be better next time."

"Next time?" I gasped.

"You know I got you hooked," she joked. "You will be back. Take care now." Then she turned around to talk to another group coming her way. I went back to my bike to wipe it down.

"How do you feel?" Lisa asked.

"Are you trying to kill me?" I replied.

"Of course not, silly. But you are quite the glutton for punishment."

After cleaning off our bikes, we made out way out of the studio and toward the basketball area. I took a look inside and saw two youth games going on.

"You know they finish up in thirty minutes," she suggested. "Open court afterward."

"No," I replied. "I don't know if I can even run after an hour of cycling class."

"Don't worry. Me neither. Besides, PowerCore class starts in about ten minutes."

"Another class? Damn, how much punishment do you need?"

"This is the most I do all week." Then she winked at me and said, "Wanna join me?"

"I'll pass. I'll do some lifting upstairs. Next time, you and I have to do something a lot less strenuous."

"Next time?"

I watched the look on her face light up with interest. "Yes. Next time. I'm thinking a place where we can sit down, dressed in something other than workout clothes. There will be food, drink, and casual conversation. No bikes, no basketball, and no gym."

"That sounds nice," she replied. "But not this weekend."

"Okay. You busy this weekend?"

"Yep," she said. Then she gave me a wicked smile and cracked, "I'll be getting ready to kick your ass in baseball. I want to be able to see you next week and savor my victory."

"You're a confident one, aren't you?"

"You're going down, buddy," she said as she poked me in the chest.

"Since you're so sure," I replied. "How about a bet? Dinner. Loser pays."

She shook her head in amazement at my proposal but then boldly stuck her hand out. "You're on." We shook hands to seal the deal. "I gotta go. You sure you don't want to do PowerCore?"

"Nope. You have fun."

She let go of my hand and went on her way. As she left, I watched her walk toward the studio where her class would be. As she got to the door, she looked back at me and waved. When she walked inside, I started to make my way upstairs to lift.

"Well, Damon," I said to myself. "You may be right. It's time to fix myself a plate."

{ 20 }

I really felt the effects of my workout as soon as I got home. My legs were so tight that the only way I could get around the house was in a slow, stiff-legged walk. I made my way to my bedroom, dumped my workout clothes in the hamper, and changed into a T-shirt and shorts. I was about to head downstairs to the kitchen when the sight of a business card lying in the middle of clutter on my dresser caught my attention. I reached over to pick it up and saw Sheila's number there. I hadn't called her since we met at the baseball game but as I flipped over the card, I remembered the note she wrote down. So I decided to give her a call.

After four rings, I heard a voice answer.

"Hello?" she responded.

"Sheila?"

"Yes."

"This is Chris. We met at the baseball game the other night and..."

"Chris! Hi! I am so glad to hear from you. How are you?"

"Right now, sore," I replied as I sunk down on the bed. I let out a quiet groan as my head reached the pillow. "Hard workout at the gym."

"Uh oh. What did you do?"

"I got talked into a cycling class, and then I lifted."

She laughed and then said, "Oh boy. You were asking for trouble."

"Tell me about it. How are you doing?"

"Fantastic. My questions are done for my class' third exam. So tonight, I'm relaxing with a nice glass of wine by my side."

"Good for you." I adjusted myself on the bed, so I was sitting up by the headboard. "Well, I called because I wanted to see what you were up to."

"Oh, I really want to get out of the house this weekend. Enjoy the sunshine before having to hunker down for the home stretch."

"I figured that."

"What do you mean?"

"You wrote that down on the back of your card when we met."

"Oh my goodness!" she replied. "Did I?"

"Yeah, you did."

"Look at me being so forward. Well, what do you have in mind?"

Thinking about the two tickets Mr. Drake gave me, I asked, "How about jazz at the museum?" I heard her groan on the other end, and I responded, "Sounds like you're not a jazz person."

"Not really. If it's classical, I'm there. Tell you what, how about Sunday brunch?"

"I can do that. I know the rooftop on Eighth is open for brunch. How about there on Sunday at eleven?"

"Let's do it! Well, I'm going to get off of here and get back into my book."

"That's cool. Enjoy the rest of your quiet night."

"Thanks. See you on Sunday."

"Take care."

Setting a date with Sheila was great, but I was still sitting on a couple of tickets to the museum. I was thinking about who else I could call when my house phone rang. I groaned because I had to limp my way downstairs to grab the landline. I couldn't get it in time, and after the fifth ring, my answering machine picked up. Then a familiar voice began to speak.

Hi Chris. It's Lydia from the bookstore. I normally don't look up a customer's information off of our mailing list. But...I don't exactly see you as the typical customer and...

"I thought I was dangerous," I said as I picked up the phone.

"Oh my God!" she replied. "I wasn't expecting you to...oh my goodness. You must think I'm crazy."

"Crazy? Nah. But it's interesting. What's up?"

"I don't know. I was just thinking about you, that's all. You know, saying goodbye in the parking lot and all."

"Why? Nothing happened." Then I heard her laughing again on the other end. "Unless you wanted something to happen."

"No, no," she frantically responded. "I don't...I...damn it. Chris, there's something about you. I see why Stacie thought so much of you."

"Let's just cut to the chase. You want to get together outside the bookstore?"

"Yes! That would be good."

"Okay. How about the museum on Saturday night?"

"For the jazz event? I thought that was sold out."

"Don't worry. I got tickets. Wanna go?"

"That would be so awesome."

"Well, I'll pick you up at..."

"No. How about I just meet you there?"

"You don't have to do that. I can..."

"No," she insisted. "I'll meet you there."

"Okay," I replied. "Show starts at seven. Meet at six thirty?"

"Deal."

"Cool. Well, see you Saturday."

"Saturday," she replied. Then her voice quieted as she said, "Chris, I hope you don't..."

"I don't," I assured her. "Just as long as you don't..."

"Chris, I don't. Have a good night."

"You too."

I hung up the phone. I leaned against the kitchen counter, still pondering Lydia's surprising call. But I was satisfied that now I had someone to go with me to the concert.

{ 21 }

Looking for a good steakhouse to go to. After last night, you better get your credit card ready.

Lisa's message on my phone woke me up on Saturday morning. I wanted to sleep in but I forgot to put my phone on vibrate. Instead, the sound of blaring horns filled my bedroom.

I rolled out of bed, grabbed my phone, and stumbled to my computer in another room down the hall. I shook my mouse to get the screen to appear and then went to our league home page. As I scanned over our matchup, I quickly saw why Lisa sent the text.

"Holy shit!" I said to myself as I looked over the results. Her team went nuts the previous night. Five of her players hit home runs, two of her starters earned victories, and three relievers got saves. The score was seven to two, and it wasn't looking too good on my side.

I was about to send her a reply when my phone rang. I checked the screen and saw that Damon was calling.

"What's up, man?" I answered.

"Not much. What about you?"

"Just woke up. Checking my fantasy baseball team."

"You winning?"

"Shit no," I replied. "It's gonna cost me a steak dinner, too."

"To who?"

"This chick that's in my league. We're playing against each other this week, and we bet a dinner on it."

"For real?" he perked up. "Hold up. You starting to fix yourself a plate?"

"I don't know. We've been talking at the gym and..."

"Go ahead, Chris! Make your move, boy."

"Look, I just..."

"Stop it!" he replied. "I can hear you already trying to downplay this. Chris, let me ask you something. Did you make the suggestion?"

"What? For dinner?" I replied. "Yeah."

"Good boy!" he cheered. "So she agreed to dinner. Work it out, and next thing you know..."

"Damon!" I shouted. "This isn't about fucking!"

"Did I say fucking?" he shot back. "Did I say that? Did the word 'fuck' come out of my mouth?"

"Why are you so animated? I'm just saying..."

"Chris, you're worried about trying to outdo me," he said.

"No, I'm not."

"Yes, you are. What did I tell you? Fix your own plate. Fix... your...own...plate." There was a pause and then he quickly blurted out, "You still got that book I gave you?"

"What book?" I answered.

"The one with all the numbers. I gave it to you when Angela and I got serious."

"Um," I pondered. "I think so."

"Throw it away."

"Do what?" I replied in surprise. "Throw it away? You gave it to me."

"I know I did. That's because I didn't need it anymore. Now you don't either. Remember Linda?"

"Linda," I huffed. "I remember that shit."

"Now go get yours. That book is past tense. Time to get into the future."

"Okay, okay," I replied. "I'll do it."

"Good deal. Chris, you know you're my dude, right? I want the best for you." Then he snapped at me, "But I will get in your ass if you don't fuck this chick."

"Come on, man. Now you said the word 'fuck'. Is it always about fucking with you?"

"It's not always about fucking," he joked. "But fucking is in the equation. Look, she sent you a text on Saturday morning to bust on you. Come on, man. She likes you."

"Damon..."

"Make it work. Jump in the damn water and swim."

"I'll handle this. Can I at least do that? Anyway, I gotta go. I got a long ass weekend."

"What's going on?" he asked.

"I gotta get shit done today so I can go to this jazz concert tonight. Then I got a brunch date tomorrow morning."

"Hold up, man!" he replied. There was a pause on the phone, and then he said, "Listen to you, Chris. A text this morning and two dates this weekend? Chris, you got this. They're falling on your head like rain."

"Damn it!" I blurted out.

"What?"

"Tony said the same shit. What is it about fucking rain?"

"Because that's what happens. You meet one, and then another shows up. Then another and another and another. Look, it's not about fucking all of them. I didn't fuck all of those girls in that book. But we met, we talked, we hung out, and we had a good vibe. Chris, stop worrying about the 'right one'. Do your thing, and she'll pop out from the rest. But get your ass out there!"

"Okay," I replied. "I will."

"You better."

"I will!"

"There you go," he cheered. "Okay, I gotta run. Angela will be back from Zumba class soon enough and I promised I would have breakfast ready."

"Damon's cooking breakfast?" I joked. "Holy shit. Should I call the fire department now or wait after you're done?"

"Man, fuck you," he replied as he laughed out loud. "I'm out. Peace."

"Out."

I hung up with Damon and turned my attention back to the computer with my fantasy baseball results. Then I picked up my phone and replied to Lisa's text.

I'll find a good steakhouse. But keep you credit card ready. The week's not over yet.

{ 22 }

The museum parking lot was packed that evening, and I ended up grabbing one of the last spots on the top level. I made my way down the lot stairs and towards the front entrance. Even in the distance, I could see multitudes of people milling around on the other side of the glass doors.

"Hey!" I heard a female voice call out.

I turned around and saw Lydia briskly walking toward me. I marveled at how she looked, a far cry from when I saw her at the bookstore. Her hair hung down to her shoulders, and she was wearing an outfit that showed off a nice set of curves.

"Hey yourself," I responded.

"I saw you when you pulled in," she said as she approached. "I was trying to catch up with you in the lot."

"No problem. You caught me." I leaned in and gave her a kiss on the cheek. She responded with a tight hug, wrapping her arms around me, and gripping my upper back. I stepped back and held her hand high, letting her take a spin to allow me a full view of her.

"You look great," I said.

"Thanks," she replied. "A little different from the bookstore?"

"Yeah, you could say that. So, are you ready for some good jazz?"

"Absolutely." She grabbed hold of my arm as we walked toward the entrance. "You know Elle's opening."

"Really?"

"I told her I was coming with you, and she was ecstatic. She's looking forward to seeing you again."

"Same here. She's a really good singer."

"Not like that, silly," she replied as she tugged my arm. "You know what I mean."

"What do you mean?" I asked. We got to the front door, and I reached out to open it for her. She walked in, and I followed, leading her to where the ticket attendant was standing. I handed over the tickets, and she pointed us to the front foyer. "Are we still on that dangerous thing you brought up?"

She laughed and then replied, "Oh that. Maybe not. But I do think you're intoxicating."

"Intoxicating?" I pondered. "That's a new one right there."

Then my cell phone buzzed in my pocket. So I reached in and pulled it out. I saw that Sheila had texted me.

I need to take a rain check on brunch tomorrow. Family emergency. I'll get with you later to set something else up.

"Another one of your women?" Lydia joked.

I laughed at her response and then replied, "What makes you think that?"

"I told you already."

"Hey guys." I looked up and saw Elle approaching us with her signature red hair and outfit. She greeted both of us with a hug and an air kiss. "Glad you could make it out."

"Well, thank this guy," Lydia said as she pointed to me. "He's the one who got the tickets."

"She called me at the right time," I added. "I thought I was going to have to eat one of these."

"Doesn't matter," Elle said. "You're here, and you're going to enjoy the show. The headliner, Albert Dennis, is a hell of a singer."

"And so are you," I said.

"Thank you," she replied sweetly as she brushed my arm.

"Guys," Lydia butted in. "I'll be right back. There's a couple I need to speak to real quick."

"Sure," I said. Then she slid over to a middle-aged couple who seemed pretty excited to see here. They each gave her a warm hug, and they chatted cheerfully.

"So what's going on with you two," Elle asked.

"Nothing," I replied. "I had tickets. She called me up on a whim, and I asked if she wanted to come with me."

"You think..." she said as she nodded over to her.

"Heck, no," I replied with a laugh. "She told me she thought I was dangerous...and too intoxicating."

Elle laughed along with me. Then she leaned in and whispered. "You're too much man for her anyway."

"What are you talking about?"

"You would tear her apart. But you know..."

I looked at her skeptically as she gave me a wink. She reached for my hand and gave it a gentle squeeze.

"I had to catch up with them," Lydia said as she came back to where we were. "They come in the bookstore all the time, and they are such a sweet couple."

"Well, I need to get ready," Elle said. "Great seeing you both."

"You, too. Have a great show."

"Thanks. Bye." Elle left for the auditorium as Lydia and I looked around at the crowd. Then I happened to look over her shoulder. Elle had stopped a few feet from us, standing right behind Lydia's viewpoint. She stared right at me, put her hand up to simulate a phone, and mouthed silently, "Call me."

The gesture caught me by surprise, and I was wondering if I was seeing what I saw. I nodded my head to acknowledge her. She smiled and winked back at me before going on her way.

{ 23 }

Elle sang with her band and got a standing ovation from the crowd. The headliner was a New Orleans-based quintet and had the crowd dancing in the aisles by the time their set was done. It took a while to exit the museum as the crowd hung around well beyond the last number, still energized from the performance.

Lydia and I finally made our way out of the museum and to the parking lot. She had a skip in her step as she walked a little in front of me. I thought about trying to keep up, but I decided to hang back for a second.

"That was so good!" she said to me as she turned around. "Elle was awesome as always, but that band after her, I couldn't sit still. I was dancing in my seat most of the time."

I started laughing before I replied, "I know. I could feel you elbow me throughout the set."

"Oops! I'm sorry." She retreated back to me and wrapped her arm around my waist. I draped my arm across her shoulder as my hand hung over in front of her. She grabbed it and locked in her fingers with mine. "Forgive me?"

"Of course. You were having a good time, and I can't be mad about that."

We got to the deck and made our way to our cars. She was parked about four spaces away from mine. When we got to her car, she unlocked herself from me. She faced me and grabbed my hands.

"Thanks for a great night," she said.

"No problem," I replied. "Thanks for coming out."

There was a long moment of silence between us. She started to fidget as she stood there holding my hands. I smiled back at her as I watched this spectacle.

"What's the matter?" I asked. "Too dangerous or too intoxicating?"

"No...yes...no," she tried to reply, stumbling over her answer. She dropped my hands and took a step back, laughing to herself. She looked back at me with a shy smile on her face. "You are so hard to resist."

"Then go for it."

"No!" she cracked back playfully. "I'm going home before I get in trouble."

"Nothing's wrong with trouble," I joked.

She laughed harder when I said that. Then she controlled herself and said, "Come here." I stepped to her, and she took my face in her hands. After holding it there for a moment, she turned my head to the side and kissed me on the cheek. "You get home safe."

"I will. You too." I wrapped my arms around her waist and hugged her. She returned the favor by grabbing onto my shoulders and squeezing herself tightly to me. We let go, and she stepped away from me. She then waved goodbye and drove off. I walked over to my car and started heading home.

When I got home, I went upstairs to change into a T-shirt and shorts. As I started to change, I thought about the text that Sheila sent me. I grabbed my phone from the dresser, found her text, and sent her a reply.

No problem. Do what you need to do, and we'll try again.

Then the sight of Elle's business card sitting on the dresser caught my eye. I grabbed her card and took a seat on my bed. I spent a few moments looking over the number, wondering if I should call her. Finally I picked up my phone and dialed her number. It rang a few times and then her voicemail picked up.

Hi. This is Elle. Leave me a message, and I'll get back to you. Bye.

I heard the beep, and then I said, "Elle. This is Chris. You told me at the museum to give you a call, so...here I am. Give me a call when you get a chance. 555-3253. Bye." I took a deep breath and my shoulders dropped. I got up and shuffled over to my dresser and put both items there. I took a long look in my mirror and the reflection staring back at me.

"Oh well," I said in resignation. "It was a try." I stepped away from the mirror and went down the hall to log into my computer.

But as soon as I turned on my computer, my cell phone rang. I quickly made my way back to my bedroom. I picked up the phone and recognized Elle's number.

"Hello," I said.

"Hey. It's Elle."

"Hey yourself. What's up?"

"Just returning your phone call. Sorry I didn't answer when you called."

"No big deal. Good show, by the way."

"Thanks. Glad you enjoyed it."

There was a long pause between us as I could hear her on the other end take a long, slow breath as she fumbled around wherever she was sitting. I finally asked, "So no after-party?"

"No after-party," she replied. "Just me at home with a glass of merlot and relaxing to some Miles." Then she took a deep breath and whispered, "But I do hate drinking alone."

I didn't immediately respond when she said the last sentence. But when it registered, it caught me by surprise. I didn't quite know what to say. Then I blurted out, "You want some company?"

I could hear a slight laugh on her end and then silence. Then question lingered in the air, and I was starting to wonder what in the world she was thinking.

"Sure," she finally said. "Come on over. I'll pour you a glass."

"Where do you live?"

"On Monument. Fourteen hundred, apartment two."

"Got it. I'll see you soon."

"Okay. See you."

I hung up on the call and immediately changed out of my shorts and into a pair of blue jeans. I slipped on my sneakers, grabbed my keys and wallet, and started downstairs. Then I stopped midway on the steps as a thought popped into my head.

"Wait a minute," I said to myself. "Just in case." I ran back upstairs and headed to the bathroom. I went into the closet and found my box of condoms. I grabbed one, thought for a second, and then grabbed another. I shoved one into each side of my wallet sleeves and then headed out.

{ 24 }

Driving to her place was easy, but parking wasn't. There was no lot where her apartment was, and the side streets were filled with cars. But lucky for me, a car pulled out of its spot about a half block from where she lived. There was just enough space for me to parallel park, so I slipped in, parked and locked the car, and headed to her place. When I got to the entrance, I saw Elle standing there, wearing only a long black bathrobe.

"Hey," she said as she opened the door. "I figured I'd pop out and see when you were coming."

"Thanks," I said as I walked in. "Good to see you. But...no red, I see."

"Only when I sing, Chris." I leaned in to kiss her on the cheek but she turned my head to where we were face to face, mere inches from each other. "Hon, we're not in public anymore." Then she slowly kissed my lips before wrapping her arms around my neck. She then let go, grabbed my hand, and led me into the apartment.

Her space was small but cozy. The living room had a couch on one side and an entertainment area on the other with a dark shaggy carpet covering the floor. There were pictures hung up all around of jazz musicians along with a shelf of CDs to the side. There was a single lamp on in the corner. We sat down on the couch where in front of us was her coffee table with two glasses of wine sitting there.

"You had a glass ready for me," I observed.

"I told you I would," she cooed. She raised her glass and said, "Cheers." I raised mine with hers and then took a sip.

"So what's the deal with red?" I asked.

"Signature look," she replied. "I got the idea from an author speaking during her book signing. Her signature look was her pink hat. She admitted she hated pink, but she needed something to stand out from other authors. I thought that was a great idea, so I decided to choose red as mine."

"Even with the hair?"

"The hair?" she replied after taking another sip from her glass. "I may have gone a bit overboard with that. I think I'll back off the next time I dye it. Maybe an auburn or something like that."

"I think that would look good." I took a sip from my glass and said, "You know, I had my doubts about calling you tonight."

"Why? I'm a good girl," she replied, smiling behind her glass.

"You are. But I was with Lydia and..."

"I know you were with Lydia. But I know you're too much man for her to handle."

"Lydia? Why do you think that?"

Elle put her glass down and leaned back into her seat. "She's a sweetie, but she's dreaming of Prince Charming coming to save her. I think you're hungry for a lot more than that."

She took my glass out of my hand and set it next to hers. She then got up from her seat and stood in front of me. She undid the knot of her bathrobe and peeled it off of her shoulders. The bathrobe dropped to the floor, revealing Elle in all of her nakedness. I marveled at her body and all of her soft curves.

"C'mon Chris," she said softly. "You think I wanted you to come over to just talk and drink wine?" She straddled me and kissed me deeply. My hands ran down her back and gently tapped her butt. As we continued to kiss, she wrapped her hand around the back of my head to pull me closer. I squeezed her butt tight, and I could hear her moan as we kissed. She pulled away from me and started to tug at my shirt. "Take this off."

I slid my shirt off and pressed my bare chest to hers. She wrapped her arms tightly around me and kissed me again.

"This is a nice encore," I said.

"Glad you're enjoying it," she cooed. "But there's a lot more to come."

She kissed her way from my lips down to my crotch, stopping along the way with a lick here and a bite there. She perched herself on her knees in between my legs. I started to reach for my belt buckle but she gently slapped my hand away. She undid it herself and then unzipped my zipper. Pulling apart my pants button, she spread the fabric to expose my boxer briefs with my erection bulging out of them.

"This is nice," she said as she rubbed her hands up and down my crotch area.

"Here," I replied as I tried to reach down to take my pants off. "Let me…"

"No," she quietly said as she put a hand on my chest. "Let me."

I laid back on the couch as she reached down and began to slowly take off my clothes. She took off my shoes and socks and put them to the right of her. Then she slid my pants off and put them to the left. I couldn't sit back any longer, so I eagerly rose up and quickly slid off my briefs. Seeing my action made her laugh slightly, but then she motioned for me to recline back. She grabbed my balls in one hand and softly stroked my dick with the other. I looked up, and her eyes locked onto mine.

"You like?" she asked.

"Oh yeah," I answered.

"Good." Then she took turns kissing the tip and the shaft of my dick, still keeping her eyes locked on mine. Then she sucked me a few times, making me moan each time she went down.

"Fuck, that's good," I panted. I rose up from my seat, grabbed her head, and kissed her.

"Hold on," she whispered. She leaned over to where my pants were and started fishing through them.

"What are you doing?" I asked.

"Looking for your wallet." Then she reached into my back pocket and found it. She felt the outline of the condoms poking through each side. "That's what I thought. You didn't come over to talk and drink wine, either."

"I didn't know what to expect. I figured I'd be prepared."

"That's fine," she said as she took one out and placed my wallet on the side. "I'm glad you came prepared. I do want you inside me." She ripped open the pouch, took the condom out, and said, "Watch this." She then put the condom in her mouth. She went down on me and when she came up, the condom was perfectly placed.

She got up from her knees and straddled over me, holding me in her hand. Then she sank down on my crotch. The feeling of me going inside her caused me to close my eyes and tilt my head back. She grinded her hips back and forth on me, bringing forth heavy breaths and her biting her lower lip. I tried to rise up but she gently pushed me back on the couch.

"Slow down, big boy," she said. "You got me all night." Then while still rocking her hips, she leaned forward and kissed me. "Don't rush it while Miles is playing."

{ 25 }

I walked into the office on Monday morning feeling refreshed. I shuffled by Shelley as she was pouring herself some coffee. She looked like she was still trying to wake up.

"Good morning, Shelley," I greeted her cheerfully.

"What's so good about it," she grumbled.

"Uh oh. What happened?"

"The in-laws were in town." She finished fixing her coffee and turned to me. She gently put her hand on my arm and said, "I love my husband. I really do love that man, but his mother drives me nuts."

"What's so bad about her?"

"Nag, nag, nag," she replied as she stepped away from me. "Just picks on everything. Geez." Then she took a deep breath and smiled. "But I'm not thinking about that anymore. I survived. They're back home, and I'm going to have a good morning."

"I hope so, too."

Then Mr. Drake walked in with his empty mug. He had a wide smile on his face.

"Mr. Drake," I said. "How was your trip?"

"It was excellent," he replied. "The weather was beautiful, and it was good to see the family. How was the concert?'

"It was great. Thank you very much for the tickets."

"You are very welcome. I hope you took a nice young lady with you."

I watched the smile on Shelley's face, and I knew she was looking for a tidbit to gossip about. I looked back at Mr. Drake and smiled.

"A friend of mine was available," I replied. "It was nice to hang out with her."

"Sounds like a good date," Shelley cut in.

"A friend of mine," I reiterated with a slight emphasis. "Was available."

"You're no fun," she joked.

"Oh, he'll be fine," Mr. Drake said as he slapped me on the back. "Chris, I'm glad you enjoyed yourself. You two have a good day." He walked off to his office, leaving Shelley and I at the station.

"Okay, let me check on my team," I said. "Have a good one."

"You too, Chris," she replied.

I made my way over to my group's cubicles. I saw everyone standing outside talked amongst themselves.

"Good morning," I said. "Did I miss the memo on the meeting?"

"Of course not," Renee replied. "Just talking about gardening."

"Gardening?" It's that time of year again, isn't it?"

"It sure is," May said cheerfully. "Time to get outside and enjoy Mother Nature."

"Sounds like fun," I said. "But I'll leave you green thumbs to talk amongst yourselves. I need to check in."

I walked away from the group and headed to my cubicle. I sat down and fired up the computer. That's when my cell phone buzzed in my pocket. I pulled it out and saw that Lisa had sent me a text.

I so fucking hate you lol. I can't believe you came back and beat me.

As soon as I logged in, I went on the Internet to the website for our fantasy baseball league. And sure enough, the Saturday deficit got turned around to a victory for me. I laughed out loud at the results, remembering the trash she was talking just two days ago. Then my cell phone buzzed again. I saw that Tony was calling me.

"What's up, man?" I answered. "What the hell are you doing up this early in the morning?"

"Early morning meeting," he replied. "They wanted us to know the news before the public announcement."

"What news?"

"Our station got bought out. We're now with All Music Radio, part of a big ass conglomerate of stations nationwide."

"Oh shit. You're not losing your job, are you?"

"Hell no. In fact, I got promoted. I'm now in digital marketing for the region."

"Congrats, man. Go ahead with yourself."

"Thanks, man. Appreciate that. You know we're celebrating at some point."

"I know. Trust me."

"Anyway, what's going on with you? What did you do this weekend?"

"Jazz concert," I said as I checked my e-mails. "Over at the museum. Took a friend of mine with me."

"A friend of yours?" he inquired.

"It's not like that," I answered. "Nothing went on with her."

"Nothing, huh?" There was a moment of silence and then he asked, "That's all you got to say?"

"Well, it isn't," I answered reluctantly. "Look, here's the deal. Nothing happened with her, but..." I got out of my seat and looked around to see if anyone was coming or was near my cubicle. Seeing that the coast was clear, I sat back down, hunched forward, and quietly continued. "But I did get with the opening act."

"What? Come on, man. The opening act?"

"Yeah. I met her before, but she wanted me to call her after the show. She invited me over to her place and...you know..."

"Damn, boy. Do your thing."

"That's not all."

"What? What else is there?"

"Look," I said as I leaned back to an upright position. "The only reason why that went down was because my Sunday brunch date cancelled."

"Hold up," he stopped me. "Let me get this straight. You took one to the museum, hooked up with another afterward, and you were supposed to have a brunch date with a third?"

"Yep. You got it. But guess what else?"

"There's more? Damn it, man. Who else?"

"You remember Lisa from the fantasy baseball league?"

"Yeah. What's going on with her?"

"We bet a steak dinner on our matchup last week."

"That's right. You did win. Nice little comeback there. But dude, I told you this was going to happen."

"What was going to happen?" I asked.

"Like rain, man," he replied. "I told you this. Now look at you. Four women got your attention this weekend. Four! Do your thing."

"I don't know, man," I said. "You're acting like I had all of this planned out."

"Man, I'm not saying that at all," he replied. "All I'm saying is that whatever you're doing, keep doing it, and ride that wave."

"Okay. I feel you." I looked at my schedule and saw I had a meeting in twenty minutes. "Look, gossip time is over. I got a meeting coming up."

"Yeah, I need to get the hell out of here as well. But we need to get together and celebrate."

"No doubt. We'll work it out. I'm out of here, man."

"Out."

I hung up my call with Tony and got ready for my meeting.

{ 26 }

I skipped working out on Monday night and decided to go on Tuesday. The parking lot was about full, and I had to park at the very back. I made my way in, and as I reached the front desk, Darrell caught my attention.

"Hey, Chris," he said. "How are things going?"

"Doing well," I replied. I reached into my wallet to pull out my gym card. He grabbed the scanner and punched me in. "Behind the counter, I see."

"I do a little of everything around here," he replied jokingly.

"Do what you gotta do."

"No doubt. Have a good workout."

"Thanks."

I walked toward the men's locker room, but out of the corner of my eye, I saw Michelle talking to a couple of people. When they walked away, she pointed in my direction and waved me over.

"You," she joked.

"What about me?"

"Get changed and go upstairs."

"What? Why?"

"Take my class," she replied softly as she playfully punched my arm. "It starts in fifteen minutes. Now get up there."

"Nah," I responded. "I don't think so."

"Come on. We have a lot of fun. Like I told you before, it's not MMA tryouts. It's a workout."

"I know..." Then she put up her fists in a boxing pose and started throwing air punches at various parts of my body. She kept her eyes on me as she smiled a wide grin. "Michelle, I'm good."

"You're no fun," she said as she stopped her motion. "I'm going to get you sooner or later."

"Yeah, right."

"I should stalk you," she joked. "Go into the directory and find out where you live. I'll just stand at your doorstep until you come to your senses."

"Or I could call the cops on your crazy ass," I fired back.

She looked at me with a funny shocked look on her face. Then she punched me in the chest. "I'm leaving you on that. But I'm going to get you one way or another."

"We'll see."

She shook her head at me before heading upstairs. I went into the locker room and got changed. I did about thirty minutes of work on the elliptical machine before heading upstairs to lift. As I walked in, I spotted Lisa lifting at the bicep curl station. I walked over to her just as she finished her set.

"You know, I was thinking," I said. "Which should I go for? A T-bone or a sirloin?"

Lisa laughed at my line before flipping my off. "I hate you."

"Is it my fault your pitchers all brought gas cans to the mound this weekend?"

"Don't remind me," she groaned. "And my two starters Sunday, five innings between the two of them. ERA and WHIPs went through the roof."

"Well, at least it's the first week," I said, offering a bit of solace.

"I know," she replied. "But I was so looking forward to seeing you pull out your credit card and pay in defeat. Tell you what. How about we meet downstairs after our workouts and head across the street?"

"Sounds like Rocky Top," I suggested.

"Yeah. How did you know?"

"They opened up last year to some great reviews. I can go for that."

"Good deal." She leaned over and reached for the handlebars to start another set. "I'll see you downstairs."

I nodded to her and made my way to the core station.

After core, I did some work on my legs. I tried to concentrate on my work, but I found myself stealing glances at Lisa. She was fully into her workout, but I saw her look over to me every now and then.

I finished up my workout, got dressed, and waited for Lisa in the café. I looked up and saw the Braves game was about to start. As I started to pay attention to the screen, my cell phone rang. I checked it and saw that it was Sheila.

"Hey, Sheila," I answered.

"Hey yourself," she replied. "Sorry I had to cancel."

"No problem. You had more important things to take care of. Everything fine?"

"Yeah. Dad had a heart scare, but it was minor. He's doing fine. So how was the concert?"

"Concert was great. Sorry you...that's right, you're not into jazz."

"Nope, not me. Now Mozart or Chopin...you got me."

"I'll keep that in mind."

"You do that," she replied. "Anyway, you free for lunch on Friday?"

"Yeah," I said in approval. "Good chance to sneak out of the office. What do you have in mind?"

"Your choice."

"Okay." I thought for a moment and then said, "How about Louie's Crab Shack in Innsbrook?"

"Oooh!" she replied in excitement. "I've heard good things about them. Sounds like a plan."

"Cool. I gotta run and get out of this damn gym."

"Sounds good. Hey, thanks for understanding. See you on Friday."

"See you later."

As I hung up my call, I saw Lisa coming out of the women's locker room. She was wearing a simple blouse, slacks, and flats while still keeping her hair in a ponytail.

"You ready?" she asked.

"Yeah," I replied. "Let's get out of here before I get caught up in this game." She looked up at the screen with me. Her face scrunched up in frustration as the batter struck out. "One of your guys?"

"Oh yeah. He sucked ass last week, too. Let's go before I get too frustrated watching this."

"Agreed."

We split apart to go to our cars. I got there in five minutes and parked near the front of the building. Lisa parked a row back and got out to meet me.

"Man, you're beating me at everything," she said.

"Hey," I replied. "Gotta keep the winning streak going." She smiled and nodded her head before punching me in the arm. "You're a feisty one, aren't you?"

"If that's what you want to call it," she said as she looked at me with a sly smile. "At least you can take it."

"I'm not afraid of you." Lisa laughed out loud before hitting me in the arm again. "Now you behave."

"Oh, I will," she replied as she wrapped her arm around my waist. "I know how to behave myself."

I opened the door for her, and we walked in. The atmosphere was bustling as waiters and waitresses bounded about serving customers.

"Welcome to Rocky Top," a young man greeted us. "How many tonight?"

"Two," I answered. Then I turned to Lisa and asked, "You want to sit outside?"

"That would be nice," she replied.

"Okay," the man said. "Follow me." He led us through the front lobby toward the patio area. He opened the door to let us out and then directed us to a table overlooking the street and the interstate. He set down two menus for us and said, "Here you are. Your waiter will be here soon to take care of you."

"Thank you," I said as we sat down. As he left, I turned to Lisa and said, "This is nice. Good choice for a victory dinner."

"Oh, shut up," she cracked back. "It's a long season and we have to play again, buster."

"Good evening," the waiter said as he came by our table. "My name is Aaron, and I'll be serving you this evening. Can I start you off with something to drink?"

"How about the six-beer sampler?" I said as I looked at my menu.

"That sounds good," Lisa added. "I'll have the same."

"Excellent," Aaron replied. "I'll be right back with your drinks."

As he went off to tend to another table, I watched Lisa stare off at the traffic.

"What's on your mind?" I asked.

"Just watching the cars drive by," she replied. Then she turned her attention to me and said, "Chris, I like you."

Her answer caught me by surprise. I jolted back slightly and gave her a curious look.

"Here are your drinks," Aaron interrupted. He then set down a sampler size of six microbrews for each of us. "Have you decided on your order or..."

"I'm ready," I said as I looked at Lisa. "I think the loser is, too." Lisa tried to kick me under the table, but her foot brushed to the side of my leg. I laughed at her effort while she scrunched her face at me. "Let me have the twelve ounce T-bone, medium well, with mashed potatoes and green beans as my sides."

"Absolutely," he replied. Then he turned to her, waiting for her order.

"You know what," she said. "I'm not going out like Mr. Manly Man over here." Her comment made Aaron and I laugh. He reached out and gave me a fist bump, causing her to shake her head in amazement. "Let me have the sirloin strips and my sides...let's do broccoli and roasted potatoes."

"Sounds good." Aaron finished writing down our orders and took our menus. "I'll be back with your orders."

As he left, Lisa raised one of her glasses and said, "Cheers." I raised one of mine with hers and then took a drink.

"That's good stuff," I said as I put my glass down. "Now, let's get back to our conversation."

"What conversation?" Then she remembered and replied, "Oh that. Chris, I do like you."

"Well, thanks."

"Chris, I mean it," she said in a more serious tone. "I like you. You can dish it as well as you can take it."

"Well," I tried to respond. "You are a lot of fun." I tried to say something more, but I couldn't find the words. Instead, I took another sip of my beer.

"Thanks," she said. "And for the record, you are way better than my ex."

"What was wrong with him?"

"He's always got pissed off when I needled him, especially when his team was playing."

"Which team was that?"

"Duke."

"Oooh," I groaned. "I know a few of those. They can be unbearable during basketball season."

"Yeah, that was him. I broke up with him right before the tournament last year. Talk about peace and quiet."

"Lisa, can I make an observation?"

"Go for it."

"You are hypercompetitive as hell. You like to stick it to a guy when you get the upper hand, and he better be ready to respond. He couldn't, and he acted out. But seriously, when do you ever let your guard down?"

The question made Lisa stop and look for an answer. She stared at me for quite some time before breaking out into a wide smile. "Guess you'll have to catch me at the right time."

"The right time?" I replied. "When is that?"

"I can't tell you. You'll have to figure it out."

{ 27 }

Dinner was delicious. My steak was cooked just right and I tore into it. Lisa was enjoying her meal as well. Along with the beer, this was a good choice for a victory dinner.

"Well," I said after I put my fork down on my empty plate. "I need to win more often."

"Oh, shut up," she cracked back. "I'm gonna get you back sooner or later."

"So how was everything?" Aaron asked as he came back to our table.

"It was great, man," I replied. "That steak was awesome."

"That's good to hear. So how about dessert?"

"No!" we both answered. We looked at each other and started laughing. Aaron smiled along with us.

"No room for dessert?" he asked again cheerfully.

"Nope," I said. "Can't do it."

"That's fine. So one check or two?"

"One," I replied with a smirk. Then I looked at Lisa.

She shot a look back at me and shook her head. Then she turned to Aaron and replied, "Fair is fair. Give it to me."

"Okay," he said. "I'll be right back."

"You bet the rest of the group like this, you may go broke," I joked.

"Oh, hell no," she replied. Then she started laughing. "Maybe Danny, but that's about it."

"So I'm the lucky one?"

"I wouldn't say luck. I just like you."

"You like doing this?"

"What's that?"

"Firing away at guys."

"It's fun."

"When do you ever stop?"

"I told you," she said as she leaned toward me. "You'll have to find out."

"Here you go," Aaron said as he came back with the check. He then handed it over to Lisa. She took out her credit card from her purse, and placed it on the tray. I sat back and smiled as she handed the tray back to Aaron.

Seeing my reaction, she silently mouthed the words "Fuck you" to me.

"I'll be right back," Aaron said.

"Let's change subjects," Lisa said as he walked off. "What about you? Any great dating stories?"

"I wish," I grumbled. "My dating life can be summed up in five words."

"Five? That's it?"

"Yep."

"What are they?"

"'You're a nice guy, but...' I've heard it from every woman I've been with."

She studied my face as she thought about my last statement. Then she said, "I don't see it."

"What?"

"I don't see it," she repeated. "'Nice guys' try way too hard. You're definitely not that type."

"Maybe Damon was right," I muttered.

"Excuse me."

"Maybe my friend was right," I said more clearly. "He told me I needed to kill him."

"Kill who?"

"The 'nice guy' in me."

"That sounds harsh," she replied. "Kill?"

"Yeah. Death to the Nice Guy."

"Here you go," Aaron said as he brought back Lisa's credit card. "I hope you have a nice evening." He then walked off quickly to tend to another table.

"That's interesting," she said as she signed the receipt. "You ready?"

I nodded, and we got up from the table. We headed back inside the main lobby to the front door. The host wished us well as I opened the door for Lisa to head out. We walked out to the lot where our cars were parked. As we got to my car, she poked in my side and said, "You better enjoy this now, buster. It's a long season."

"Yes it is," I replied. "A long season for you to fall further and further back in the pack."

She immediately slapped me on my arm. "You are so full of it. I'm leaving."

"See you later, Lisa," I replied.

I started toward my car but then I stopped to watch her got to hers. When she opened the door, she looked back at me. For a couple of moments, we just stared at each other. She nervously bit her lower lip as she looked out over the lot. Finally, she waved goodbye and drove off.

{ 28 }

Friday was the nicest weather day of the week, which made my lunch date with Sheila an extra reason to get out of the office. Around eleven thirty, I put my computer in sleep mode and headed out.

"Where are you going?" Renee asked.

"Lunch," I replied. "Gonna enjoy this nice weather."

"What's her name?" Jennifer butted in.

"What are you talking about?"

"You know exactly what I'm talking about, mister." She stepped out of her cubicle and leaned against the wall with her arms folded. The smile on her face told me she was going to keep inquiring until I told her something. Soon the rest of the team stepped out and joined her.

"Okay," April said. "I heard the commotion. What's up?"

"You should've seen him walk by here," Jennifer said. "He had a quite a bounce in his step."

"Sounds like he's going to see someone," May said in a sing-songy voice.

The mini-interrogation caught me by surprise, but I found their inquiry funny. My eyes attended to each of my team until I reached James.

"Don't look at me," he said, throwing his hands up in sur-render. "You're on your own on this."

"Gee, you're no help," I joked. Then I turned my attention to the group and responded, "Okay, I met her at a baseball game."

"Told you," Jennifer replied enthusiastically, slapping her hands together. "Now spill it."

"Oh, come on. There's nothing to spill." I looked at the faces of my group and I could tell they weren't buying it. "I met her at a VCU game, and we're going out for lunch. Can I go now?"

"I guess so," June replied. "But..."

"No," I interrupted. "No details."

"Come on, Chris," May replied.

"You have to tell us something," Jennifer added.

"Nope," I said. "I'm going to lunch."

. I started on my way once again to the front entrance and to the parking lot. I saw a few others in the building look-ing to do the same, donning their sunglasses before walking outside. I walked out of my car and drove away to Innsbrook Center where Louis' was located. I parked near the front of the lot and made me way to the restaurant. Immediately I picked out Sheila sitting at one of the outside tables. She was wearing a blue business suit and matching heels.

"Hey there," I called out. "I didn't know this was sup-posed to be a special occasion."

She laughed as she got up to give me a hug. "You're funny," she said as she sat back down. "No, we had a news conference this morning for a new project with the city."

"Aren't you the busy one?"

"Tell me about it. Class took their exams yesterday, too. Today is my day to breathe, and then I hunker down again this weekend."

"Hello," a waitress said as she approached us. "My name is Crystal, and I'll be your waitress this afternoon. Would you like to start off with a drink?"

"Just water for me," I said.

"Same here," Sheila added.

"Okay. I'll be right back," Crystal replied.

As she walked off, Sheila turned to me and said, "I am so sorry I had to cancel on you Sunday."

"No problem. You had more important things to worry about than me."

"So how was the concert?"

"It was good," I said as I checked out the menu. "Too bad you don't like jazz."

"Never have. Give me the symphony over jazz any day."

"Here are your waters," Crystal said as she put a glass in front of each of us. "Have you decided what you want to order?"

"Yes," Sheila said as she put down her menu. "I want the Maryland-style crab cakes with coleslaw and sweet potato fries as my sides."

"That sounds good," I said as I turned to Crystal. "I think I'll have the same."

"Got it," she replied. "I'll be back with your orders."

Sheila and I watched her leave our area and go back inside. Then we turned to each other. She smiled and looked away, nervously tapping her fingers on the table. I wanted to say something to her, but I couldn't seem to find the words.

"Okay," I finally said. "What's on your mind?"

"I'm glad you're here," she replied.

"I'm glad I'm here, too. But what's really on your mind?"

She looked away, pursing her lips and still tapping her fingers. Then she turned to me and grinned. She took a deep breath, leaned in, and said, "I've been thinking about you since the VCU game." Her answer caught me by surprise, causing me to lean back and try to digest the statement. Then she laughed nervously and replied, "Oh my goodness. You don't think I'm too forward, do you?"

"Of course not," I replied. "Just a little surprised."

"I have to confess. I get so wrapped up in classes, my students, publications, and whatever the hell else goes on at the university. I finally figured I need some attention for myself."

"So you put me in your crosshairs?" I joked.

"No. It's not like that. It's just that...well, I've been talking to one of my girlfriends, and she told me to get out there and start meeting guys."

"Any success?"

"You're here, aren't you?" she said with a devilish smile.

"Oh, I see," I replied. "Guess I'm glad to be a success story."

"No problem." She took a sip of water and then said, "You know, I'm also doing the online dating thing."

"How is that working out?"

"They don't understand me."

"Why not?"

Sheila took out her phone and tapped it a couple of times. Then she handed it to me and said, "Read the headline."

I looked at the screen and saw it was her online dating profile. She had her university headshot picture along with her headline. When I looked at it, my eyes popped wide open with surprise.

"An Intelligent Man's Sexual Fantasy," I read. Then I handed her the phone and replied, "Now that's putting it out there."

"Oh yeah," she said. "Why beat around the bush? Too bad most of the replies think that I'm easy."

"What do you want them to think?"

"That I'm a good woman, but I also have a naughty side." Then she leaned in and whispered, "But a man has to figure out which key opens the door."

"Which key?"

"Yes, if he's up to the challenge. But then again...if I really like him...I'll just give him the key myself."

"Keys," I replied with a slight laugh. "No wonder they don't understand you."

"Chris," she said. "I like you. Can you make me a promise?"

"Sure."

"No pressure, no expectations. Wherever this goes, that's where it goes. Let's just enjoy each moment."

"I can do that."

I reached out my hand, and she responded by clasping it in both of hers. As she rubbed it from my fingers to my wrist, she kept her attention solely on my hand. Then she looked up and said, "Nice hand. Tell me, what else is nice on you?"

"You are so bad," I replied.

That caused her to let go, lean back, and laugh out loud.

{ 29 }

Early the next morning, I headed over to Richmond Fitness. After arriving and changing, I did some time on the elliptical machine before heading upstairs. I looked over at the free weight section of the gym. Normally this area would be packed, but today I only saw a few people lifting. So I decided to work out there. As soon as I got to the weight benches, I saw Michelle there loading up a bar with weights.

"Hey," she said. She reached out and gave me a fist bump. "You're in here early."

"Didn't feel like doing anything last night," I replied. "I figured I'd get up early this morning and head here."

"I hear ya." She then loaded another two weights to the bar. "Give me a spot?"

"Sure."

She took her place on the bench as I helped lift the bar off the rack for her. She pushed through her set before putting the bar back in place. She sat up and said, "Your turn."

"What?"

"You didn't come over her to just talk, did you?"

"Well," I hesitantly replied. "Of...of course not."

"Good. Your turn."

"Okay," I said. We switched places, and I laid down on the bench as Michelle stood over me. "You do a little of everything in here."

"Have to. Different exercises work out different muscle groups. If you do the same routine over and over again, I guarantee you'll plateau."

"So I need to diversify?" I replied as I grabbed the bar and started my set.

"Sure do. Hint, hint."

"You're still on that?" I grunted as I kept lifting. I saw Michelle spotting me but keeping a grin on her face. I got through my set, and she helped me put the bar back on the rack. I got up in a seated position and said, "I haven't done that in a while."

"You just need to stay with it," she replied as we switched places. "Just make sure you save time for my class."

"You do this to all the guys, don't you?"

"Not all of them," she replied as she took her position. Her eyes caught mine, and she winked at me. She went through her set and sat up on the bench. "Okay, I gotta go."

"Already?"

"Chris, I've been here since seven. It's time to go home."

"Geez, that early."

"I got a lot to do today. I wanted to get this knocked out first thing. So you're on your own now. Don't forget about what I said."

"You are too much. What's next? Are you gonna show up at my doorstep and tell me you're not leaving until I make a promise?"

"That's a good idea!" she responded. "I'll have to keep that in mind."

"Oh goodness," I groaned.

She laughed and then gave me a fist bump. "Have a good workout." Then she ran off downstairs.

I moved on to another station and continued my workout. I lifted for another forty-five minutes before heading to the outer track. Feeling good about myself, I decided to jog around this time. So I put on my headphones and got started at a slow pace, staying on the inside track away from the faster runners. When I turned the corner, I spotted Lisa playing in a game. She pulled up for a jumper, but it came up woefully short.

"Airball!" I yelled. "Airball!"

Some of the guys looked up and started laughing. Lisa saw me and tried to brush it off but instead yelled, "Shut up!" before cracking a slight smile.

I kept going along. I felt good running, so I picked up the pace a little. I got lost in the music as I kept a steady pace. Then all of a sudden, I felt someone's foot thud into my backside. It didn't hurt but it definitely caught my attention. I turned around and saw Lisa standing there, arms crossed and smirking.

"What the hell?" I said. "Was that you?"

"No, it was Santa Claus," she joked. "Who else did you think it was?"

"So what...you decided to kick me in the butt?"

"Damn right I did. You deserved it, too."

"Why?'

"Yelling 'airball', you bastard."

"You shot it, not me," I cracked back.

She stepped closer to me and said between her smiling teeth, "You weren't supposed to say anything."

"Oh, my bad," I replied.

We walked away from the track and through the weight areas. After making out way downstairs, she playfully punched me in the arm.

"You're so violent today," I joked. "I need to get away from you."

I started to step away but Lisa grabbed my hand and pulled me closer to her.

"Hey, you know I'm just messing with you right?" she said.

"I know, but geez..." She kept my hand in hers, smiling even brighter. "Okay, you're forgiven. For now."

"Thanks, Chris," she said sweetly.

"So what are you doing today?"

"Trying to get straight for tomorrow."

"What's up?"

"Heading to Baltimore for a regional meeting. So I need to handle all of my house chores today."

"That stinks," I replied. "You wanna break away later and hang out?"

"I wish," she groaned. "But I will be dead tired after I'm done." Then she let go of my hand and turned to face me. "I do want to spend more time with you, though."

"Same here. That's why..."

"I know," she said. "We'll work on that." She looked over my shoulder and checked the clock. "I gotta get out of here. Text me later this week, and we'll work on something."

"Sounds good. See ya."

As I turned away, Lisa called out, "Hey!"

I turned around, and she quickly approached me. Then she leaned in and gave me a quick kiss on the cheek. She smiled and headed to the women's locker room, leaving me amazed at what just happened.

{ 30 }

The next week was quiet as a church mouse in my office. April and June were on vacation, and our spring and summer work hours kicked in. Many people took advantage of the chance to work a half day on Friday, and by one o'clock, just about the entire floor had cleared out.

I was finishing up a project when I heard a knock on the side of my cubicle. I turned around and saw Mr. Drake standing there.

"What are you doing here?" he asked. "I thought you'd be like the rest of the building and leave at noon."

"No, sir," I replied. "I was finishing up that regional report you asked for. It actually helped that the office was a bit quiet."

"Well, that's good." He slipped into my cubicle and sat down on the far desk. "So how's life, Chris?"

"Life is good," I said as I spun around in my chair. I leaned back and continued, "I'm actually getting out and doing things."

"Hope you got some company with you."

"Oh boy," I moaned. "You sound like my team."

Mr. Drake let out a hearty laugh at that statement. He took a moment to calm himself before he turned back to me.

"Well, I don't try to pry too much. I just hope you're out there meeting some nice young ladies. I remember not too long ago you were all out of sorts, and you thought staying at work would help the situation."

"I remember that, too. I took it out on my team and I shouldn't have."

"You live and you learn. At least you're getting out. Here's a word of advice. Meet as many women as go out as much as you can. The one for you will stand out from the rest. Trust me."

"Speaking from experience, huh?"

He leaned in said quietly, "Let's just say Mrs. Drake wasn't the only one."

"What?" I replied, surprised by his answer. "You were playing the field?"

"I dated my fair share. I actually thought this girl named Brenda Summers was going to be the one. We met during Freshman Orientation and clicked immediately."

"What happened with her?"

"She pledged a sorority. Once she got into Greek life, she vanished. But there were others. Patricia Clarke, Lisa Rows, Valerie Taylor..."

"I knew a Valerie Taylor," I interrupted. "She taught high school English. I thought something could work out with that but it didn't pan out. She moved on to another guy, they moved to Kentucky, and..."

"She's working for a local theater company?" he asked.

"Yeah," I responded. "Wait a minute. Are you telling me that the Valerie Taylor I knew is the same...?"

"Valerie Taylor? Chris Wheeler, I believe so." Mr. Drake and I had a great laugh about this discovery. "Chris, I didn't know you two were an item?"

"A little bit, Mr. Drake."

"You know she's..."

"Seventeen years older than I am. She brought that up once or twice."

"Look at you," Mr. Drake said as he shook his head in amazement. "You sly dog. You're going to be fine."

"Well," I said as I turned back to my computer. "Do you want this report this afternoon? I'm about to finish it."

"Don't worry," he answered. "I won't have time to read it this weekend. Just send it to me Monday morning."

"I'll do that," I said as I turned back to him.

"Well, I'm on my way. I'm going to finish up a couple of things and then head to the wine shop."

"Wine shop? What for?"

"My wife's got friends coming over for dinner, and she wants me to bring home a couple of bottles."

"So you're big into wine?"

"Heck no!" he answered emphatically. "I'll take beer any day of the week. Budweiser has never done me wrong. My wife is the one with the *Winery Digest* subscription. I just buy what she tells me. But Chris, you should always be ready when it's time to entertain."

"So how am I supposed to do that?" I asked.

"Just go to the local Total Wine shop, find an attendant, and ask, 'What do you recommend?' Whatever they pick is what you buy."

"Thanks, Mr. Drake. I'll keep that in mind."

"Chris," he said as he walked out of my cubicle. "Have a good weekend. I'll see you on Monday."

{ 31 }

Heeding Mr. Drake's advice, I drove from work to the wine shop. I fought through nasty traffic the whole way, a three-car accident causing the backup. I finally got through the mess and made it to Total Wine. As I was walking in, my cell phone buzzed in my pocket. I saw that it was Laura on the other line.

"Hey, stranger," I answered.

"Hey, yourself. What's up?"

"Just getting off work. I'm trying to run an errand before I go home. How's life in California?"

"The same. Beautiful weather to go along with the crazy people."

"That's funny," I responded. I looked around the store and took in the view of aisles of wine in the store. "Wow."

"What are you wowing about?" Laura asked.

"I'm in the wine shop," I said as I grabbed a mini-basket. "I didn't know they had this many choices."

"Oooh, wine," she replied with a perky voice. "Get a couple for me."

"A couple for you?"

"Yeah. Have a Merlot and a Zinfandel waiting for me."

"Yeah, right." I looked up at the sign for the Merlot bottles and walked down that aisle. "Like you're coming to town anytime soon."

"For your information, I'll be back in Richmond in two weeks."

"Get out of here," I responded. "What the hell's going on in two weeks?"

"Richmond Adult Expo."

"Adult Expo?" I asked as I looked at the row of bottles in front of me. "What in the...oh! I saw that in the news. Media around here did a couple stories on that

. So you're signed up for it?"

"They haven't made the official announcement, but yours truly will be the headline attraction."

"Go ahead with yourself, Miss Headline Attraction."

"Thanks, babe."

As I walked to the aisle for Chardonnays and Rieslings, my cell phone buzzed again. I saw that it was Elle trying to reach me. I hit the button to send her to voicemail. "That can wait."

"Who's that?" Laura inquired. "Another hot date?"

"Maybe," I replied. "She's a jazz singer."

"Oooh. You making sweet music with her?"

"Oh stop it."

Laura cracked up on the end, laughing audibly in my ear. I just nodded my head as I made my way to the regional aisle. Wines from the East Coast lined up all the way down the aisle. I looked over each tag until I found wines from Virginia.

"So, are you gonna answer me or what?"

"Okay, okay," I relented. "Look, she can sing her ass off, and she's great in bed."

"I knew it. You go, boy!"

"Will you stop it?"

"Chris, you stop it. You're downplaying yourself. I bet you rocked her world. Look, you're a strong and confident guy. You need to let it out more."

"You mean like the last time you were in Richmond?" I joked.

"Not just that, but...that night was awesome." Then I heard her groan in frustration. "Crap. I gotta get out of here."

"What's up?"

"I'm working with a friend of mine on a new script. I promised him I'd be over at the restaurant in thirty minutes."

"Well, don't let me hold you up. Great talking to you."

"You, too. Remember, two weeks. Save me some time."

"I will do that. Take care."

"Kisses."

I hung up the call with Laura and went back to making a selection. As I put back another bottle I was contemplating over, I noticed the sign for chocolate wine. The sight of that bottle intrigued me, and I waved over one of the staff walking down the aisle.

"Yes, sir," the attendant said. "How can I help you?"

"Tell me about this chocolate wine," I replied. "That's an interesting choice."

He laughed and said, "Sir, we can't keep this on the shelves. Believe me, it's a little different. But it's gotten good reviews from our customers."

"Okay," I said as I grabbed a bottle. "I'll have to try it out."

"Anything else I can help you with?"

"Actually, yes. What do you recommend for a good Merlot and a Zinfandel?"

{ 32 }

I started my work week at the Convention Center man-
ning our company table at the area Retail Expo. Shelley had
grabbed me first thing Monday morning and talked me into
helping out. I would've normally found a way to get out of
committing, but with a promise of a free lunch, I decided to
pitch in. The expo ate up three days of the week, but it was
actually nice to be out of the office.

I didn't get back to the gym until Thursday, and after
the places Shelley took the team to lunch, I needed a good
workout. I changed into my workout gear and worked up a
good sweat on the treadmill. I made my way upstairs to the
weights to start lifting. But before I could sit down, I felt an
arm wrap around my back. I looked to my left and saw Lisa
holding on to me with a wide smile on her face.

"Hey there," she said cheerfully. "Haven't seen you in a
bit."

"Retail expo," I replied. "Now I need to work off those
business lunches."

"I hear you. We had one of those today as well."

There was quiet between the two of us as Lisa's smile
grew a bit wider. Then it hit me why she was being so friendly.

"I'm not trading Freeman," I said with a chuckle.

"Come on, man!" she exclaimed as she let go of me and backslapped my arm. "I need a first baseman. You got like three guys already."

"I know. But I'm not giving you Freeman. How about Martinez? He's hitting over three hundred."

"Yeah, right. The same guy who hasn't hit a home run in a month? No, I'll pass." As I made my way to the bicep curl bench, she followed right behind me. "Chris, it's a good trade."

"No," I said as I sat down and got situated. "I'm not coming off of Freeman. If you want to talk about the other two, I'm all ears. Besides, it's not my fault your guy got popped for PEDs. Why didn't you get his backup?"

"Because somebody else got him as soon as the news came out."

"That stinks." I worked through a set of reps and then leaned back on the seat. "Check the waiver wire?"

"Maybe Morrison or Bell. I don't know." Then she paused for a moment and pointed at the machine.

"Wanna work in?" I suggested.

"Might as well." We switched places, and she readjusted the weights. While lifting, she said, "I gotta figure out how I'm gonna catch up."

"What are you? Eighth?"

"Ninth," she replied as she finished her set. "You're second, aren't you?"

"Half a game out of first." We switched places again, and I reset the weights. "Don't worry. We've still got a long way to go. Besides, sixth place gets you into the playoffs. Then you know..."

"All bets are off," she finished my sentence with a smile. I went through another set of curls and then switched again with Lisa. After she finished her set, she said, "Thanks for letting me work in with you."

"No problem," I replied as I gave her a fist bump. "Got plans this weekend?"

She laughed and then said, "Oh yeah. One of Danny's friends is in town, and she invited me to tag along and hit the town. Hell if I know where we'll end up."

"Well, have fun."

"You, too." She slapped me gently on the arm and took off as I moved on to the next station.

{ 33 }

I planned on having a quiet weekend, so I got my groceries right after work on Friday and hunkered down at home. Friday night and most of the day Saturday was spent either on the couch watching TV or sitting on the floor with a PlayStation game going on.

Finally, I got a phone call on my cell Saturday evening. I saw that it was Tony on the line.

"What's up, man?" I answered as I put him on speakerphone.

"What's going on with you, big boy?" he answered back.

"Not a damn thing. Sitting at home all weekend."

"Sitting at home? What the fuck, man?"

"I'm good. Just me, the TV, and PlayStation."

"Well, get your ass out of the house and come to Top Of The World."

"What's going on out there?" I asked as I put my game on pause. I got up from the floor and sat in my Lay-Z-Boy.

"You remember I told you they changed DJs, right?"

"Yeah. I remember that."

He paused on the other end and then said, "Shit is crazy now. The music is hot, and the women are hotter, man. So get the fuck out of the house."

"Come on, man..." Then my cell phone rang. I saw that A.J. was calling. So I put the two calls together.

"Talk to me, A.J.," I said. "I got Tony on here, too."

"A.J.!" Tony called out. "Tell Chris about Top Of The World."

"Oh my God!" he replied. "You have to go out there now that they've changed things up. Man, it's crazy live in that place."

"So Chris, you are coming tonight, right?" Tony asked.

"Okay," I relented. "I'll be out there."

"Good! A.J., you coming out?"

"Yeah, man," he replied.

"Cool. First round on me when y'all get here."

"Got it," A.J. said. "Chris, see you when you get there."

"Okay. Out." I hung up the phone and groaned, "So much for a quiet weekend."

I changed outfits and headed out the door. I got to the parking lot across the street from the club in quick time and parked on the first level. When I got to Top Of The World, there was a line wrapped all the way around the building. I gazed over the crowd and realized what the guys were talking about. There were more women in line than men and just about every one of them looked good. I spotted A.J. near the middle of the crowd. I caught his attention, and he waved over to me.

"Goodness," I said as I approached. "You weren't kidding."

"Told you, man," he replied. "It's been jumping." Then he leaned in and whispered, "You like what you see?"

"Yes!" I replied quietly.

Then I looked up and saw Tony standing on the corner on his cell phone. I didn't want to yell out so I tried to wave him down. After a couple of tries, Tony looked up at our direction. He acknowledged us, hung up his call, and came over.

"Look at him," he said to me. "He thought he was going to stay inside all weekend."

"I know, man," I replied. "You were right about this place."

"Told you." Then he waved for us to come with him. "Come on. You're with me."

A.J. and I followed him to the front of the line. Tony talked to the bouncer, and he let all three of us in ahead of the line. We passed by the bar downstairs and went up the steps to where the front desk was. Tony talked to the attendant there, and then she waved for us to go through. I could hear the thumping sound of house music coming from the upper level. The bar area and pool tables hadn't changed a bit, but there were a few more tables in the area and a couple of waitresses were making the rounds serving drinks.

Tony got to the bar right where the bartender was standing. The guy was well over six feet tall with the bushiest of black beards and hair hanging well past his shoulders.

"What's up?" he called out. "What can I get for you?"

"Three Ruby Reds!" Tony replied. Then he waved us to the bar. "Come on and drink, man."

"What are you ordering?" I asked.

"Shots! I told you first round is on me. You're gonna love this."

We watched the bartender pick up a clear bottle of alcohol and pour it into a mixer, followed by red grapefruit juice and Sprite. He shook the mixer vigorously and then poured the contents into three oversized shot glasses.

"Hey, man," I called out to the bartender. "What was that bottle that you picked up?"

"The bottle?" he replied. "Oh, that's moonshine."

"Moonshine! What the hell?"

"Distillery downtown started making it a few months ago. It's pretty popular here, and the shit's actually good." Then he turned to Tony and asked, "Starting a tab?"

"Yeah," he replied.

"No problem." He then took Tony's credit card and filed it away.

"Okay!" Tony yelled out as he handed each of us a shot glass. "Let's have some fun tonight!"

"Most definitely," I replied. We clinked glasses and downed our shots. The shot was good, but the bartender was a bit strong on the moonshine. I could feel the burn from my lips to my guy, and I let out a groan when I finished. "Man, that's strong."

"Good though, right?" Tony replied.

"It's good. It's good."

"Hey, let's head to the upper level."

We headed upstairs where the DJ and the dance floor were located. There was also another bar located in the far left corner of the room. Lights were flashing on and off from the ceiling, giving off a kaleidoscope effect on the floor. The floor was packed with people dancing to the continuous sounds.

"Hey," Tony called out to us. "I'm heading up to the DJ booth. I'll get up with you later." We both nodded our heads as Tony made his way through the dance floor. I went to turn to A.J., but he had spun away to talk to a group of women that had just come in. I turned back to the floor and scanned the atmosphere. Then I saw a woman waving in my direction. I thought it was for someone else, but then I looked again and saw she was still waving. So I started through the maze of dancing people. When I got halfway there, I realized that woman was Danny.

"Hey there!" she called out as I approached her. She reached out to me and gave me a quick hug. When I stepped away, I took immediate notice to her black leather pants.

"Hey yourself," I replied. "Like the leather."

"Oh yeah," she said with a wide smile. "I haven't worn these in over a year." Then she turned to her friend who was dancing to the left of her. She was about the same height as Danny with the same body features. But her hair was a tad longer and she dressed a little plainer in a simple blouse, blue jeans, and short black heels. "Chris, this is my friend Alicia."

"Nice to meet you," I said as I reached out to shake her hand.

"Nice to meet you, too," she replied.

Then I felt a tug on my shirt. I looked over and saw Lisa there.

"And you know her, don't you?" Danny joked.

"Oh yeah," I replied. I kept viewing her from head to toe. She wore a one-piece, thigh-high black dress with matching open-toed heels. Her curves showed in all the right places and all I could do was mouth the word, "Wow." Lisa laughed at the look on my face and did a quick spin for me, so I could see the back view.

"A different look, huh?" she said.

"You definitely haven't worn that in the gym," I replied. She laughed again as she gently rubbed her hand down my arm. When her hand reached mine, I grabbed it and held on. The movement caught her by surprise. She looked at me with a curious smile on her face. She then let go of my hand and started to dance. I joined her and soon we started to slink away from the other two.

After a few songs, I glanced over at Danny, and she gave me a nod of approval. I looked back at Lisa and was enjoying seeing the sway of her body and smile on her face. Then I saw a guy work his way to Lisa and started to dance with her from behind. Her smile turned into a look of disgust as he grinded on her backside. I reached out my hands and pulled Lisa close to me. As I held her in my arms, I looked over her shoulder at him and gave him a look of disapproval. He backed off and danced off in a different direction. I looked back at Lisa and gave her a nod. I tried to step away, but she brought me in closer by wrapping her arms around my shoulders. Our tempo slowed even with the upbeat thumping of the music pounding around us.

Then I saw Danny tap Lisa on the arm. "We're going to the bar," she said.

Lisa nodded to me and said, "I gotta go with my friends. Wait for me, okay? I'll come back to you."

"Okay," I replied.

I let go of her, but Lisa kept her hands on my shoulders. She paused for a moment and then pressed her lips to mine. The action caught me by surprise, but Lisa guided her hands to my face and continued to kiss me. She finally pulled herself away, smiled, and gave me a quick wave before she went off with her friends. I stood motionless on the floor as the crowd continued to dance around me.

{ 34 }

Lisa and I danced together the entire night. When the last song played and the main lights came on, she looked at me with a bit of disappointment that the club was about to close. She then smiled at me, reached out, and gave me a long hug.

"Thanks for dancing with me," she whispered in my ear.

"Same to you," I replied. "That was fun."

She let go of me and nodded in approval.

"Hey guys," Danny said. "Looked like you two were having a ton of fun."

"Well, I'm not used to seeing her in anything but gym clothes," I replied.

"The same to you, buddy," Lisa cracked back as she back-slapped my arm. "But I can get used to seeing you like this."

"Same here."

"Have a good night, everybody!" the bouncer called out from behind the crowd. "Make your way toward the exit, people! Have a good night!"

As we started toward the exit, I reached down and grabbed hold of Lisa's hand. She immediately locked her fingers in mine, and as I looked over at her, she smiled and leaned her head on my shoulder. Danny and Alicia were walking ahead of us, paying us no mind. We made out way downstairs and out into the street. Some people were milling around the exit, while others walked away in different directions.

"Wow," Alicia said. "That was awesome, but that wore me out. Can we call it a night?"

"I'm with you, girl," Danny replied. Then she turned to me and said, "Chris, it's been fun, but we gotta go."

"Well, it's good to see everyone. Nice to meet you, Alicia."

"Same to you, Chris. Have a good night."

Then I turned to Lisa. "You better get these two home."

"Yeah, I guess so." She let go of my hand and patted me on the back before moving in front of me. "Thanks for a fun night," she said while running her index finger down my chest.

"You, too. Enjoyed dancing with you."

"Come here," she said as she motioned for me to come closer. She leaned in and gave me a quick kiss followed by a longer one. She pulled away from me and said, "I'll see you at the gym."

"Absolutely," I replied. I waved to the two others as I headed to my car. But after walking a few steps, I looked back and saw Lisa looking back at me while walking away.

As I drove off to go home, I tried to listen to the radio but I couldn't concentrate on the music. My mind was fixated on Lisa. The way she looked at me and the way she danced was all I could think about.

I got home and once I got inside, I quickly checked my phone to see if anyone had called. Seeing no messages, I went upstairs and changed out of my wardrobe. I sat down at the edge of my bed and looked around my room. Even at this late hour, I was still energized from my club. So I decided to take a quick shower and head back downstairs to watch TV.

I turned to SportsCenter and the first highlight that came up was a Braves win on a walk-off home run. Just as the player stomped on home plate amid a sea of exuberant teammates, my cell phone rang.

I looked and saw it was Lisa.

"Hey there," I said.

"Hey," she answered quietly. "You up?"

"Yeah. Just watching SportsCenter. Get everybody home?"

"Yeah." There was a long pause before either of us said anything. "I had fun tonight."

"Me, too."

There was another long pause. I was about to say something when she blurted out, "Chris, can I ask you something?"

"Sure," I replied as I sat up in my seat.

"Do you...do..."

"Do what?"

"Nothing...nothing. Tonight was just wild and...I...I don't feel like turning in."

"Do you want to come over?"

"Do you mind?" she answered hesitantly. "If you're about to call it a night, I totally understand and..."

"Lisa," I stopped her. "I'm not turning in anytime soon. Come on over. Where are you now?"

"Well, I'm coming down Boulevard just past Broad."

"You're not too far away. Just get to the interstate, take..."

"Hey," she interrupted. "Just give me your address. I'll put it in my GPS."

"No problem. Ten eleven Holly Oak Lane."

"Got it. See you in a bit."

"Okay. See ya."

I hung up on the call and sunk back into my seat, surprised by what just transpired. I tried to get back to the program on TV but the thought of Lisa coming over had me nervous. I got up and paced around the living room every few moments in anticipation. If I wasn't pacing the living room, I was pacing the kitchen.

Then the door bell rang. I stood in silence as I looked in the direction of the front door. I knew it was her, but I couldn't move. Finally I started slowly walking through the living room and down the hall. After taking a deep breath, I opened the door, and there was Lisa standing there, still in her clothes from the club.

"Hey," she nervously said.

"Hey yourself," I answered quietly. "Come on in."

She walked in, and I closed the door. We stood in the hallway facing each other. She fidgeted in her stance as I leaned against the other wall with my legs feeling uneasy. Finally I took a step toward her. She took a deep breath and opened up her arms to welcome me in. I leaned in and kissed her. As our lips touches, the tension in our bodies lifted. She wrapped her arms tightly around my neck as I held my hands around her waist.

As our kisses drew deeper and longer, I could feel her hands venture from my neck all along my back. I pulled her in closer and gripped the small of her back with one hand while my other ran up and down her spine. When I found the zipper at the back of her dress, she loosened her grip on me in anticipation of what was to come.

I started to unzip her, making my way to the bottom of her skirt. I pulled the dress away from her shoulders and let it fall to the floor, leaving her wearing only her black lace bra and matching thong panties. I ran my finger from the center of her chest to her navel and I could feel her body shudder ever so slightly.

Then I looked at her and said, "Let's go upstairs."

She nodded her head in approval. So I took her hand and led her upstairs to my bedroom. At the edge of the bed, I kissed her again. Her hands worked their way inside my shirt, and I could feel her fingernails rake up and down my back.

"You've got too many clothes on," she suggested as she pulled away from me. So with her guiding me, I took my shirt off and stood before her. She leaned down and kissed me on random parts of my chest. I reached behind her and found the clasp of her bra. I got it undone and she stood up so I could take it off. I could feel the contrast of her soft breasts and hard nipples in my hands. She smiled at me as I continued to explore her chest. Then I picked her up and placed her on the left side of the bed. I slowly took her heels off before crawling over to the other side.

As she turned toward me, we kissed. My hand started down her chest again and continued to her crotch. She spread her legs willingly as I rubbed the outside of her panties. Then my hand gently moved inside and I felt she was wet with excitement. I started to rub her pussy and with that action, her lips pulled from mine. She closed her eyes and let out a long, gentle purr. She then fell on her back, and as my pace increased, her hips rocked to the rhythm. Her breaths grew shorter and her moans got louder. Then her back arched up, and I watched her close her eyes and put her hand over her mouth to keep her noises down.

I pulled her hand away and whispered in her ear, "Don't worry. You can be as loud as you want."

She stayed with her mouth open and her eyes closed until she loudly panted through her orgasm before letting out a long, drawn out moan. She opened her eyes and grabbed my hand to pull it away, trying to catch her breath in the process. After she collected herself, she pulled her face to mine and kissed me.

She kept her eyes locked on me as she kissed her way down my chest to my stomach. She rested her head there as her hand moved underneath my shorts and gently grabbed my erection. I pushed my shorts off as she stroked me with one hand and grabbed my balls with the other. My head fell back on the pillow as I felt her mouth on the head of my dick. She alternated between sucking and kissing, causing me to moan ever so slightly. Then she moved her way up to me and kissed me while still stroking my erection.

As we pressed our foreheads together, I whispered, "I wanna be inside you." She nodded in approval and I laid her on the bed. I gently removed her panties, reached into the drawer of the lamp stand, and pulled out a condom. After I put it on, I moved in front of her and she opened her legs.

She gasped as I entered her as her wetness allowed me in easily. I pumped in and out of her as our bodies connected in the act. She gently raked her fingernails up and down my back as our eyes locked into each other. Then she reached for the back of my head and pulled me in for a deep kiss. I quickened my pace, causing her to pull away and let out a loud moan.

"Oh God, Chris!" she panted in pleasure. "Fuck me!"

I started to feel my orgasm building, and I kept going as her moans and groans got louder. Finally, I couldn't hold it in anymore.

"Oh my God!" I grunted.

"Come for me," she replied while stroking the sides of my face. "Go for it."

Then as I came into my condom, I let out a guttural scream as I stayed inside her. When the feeling subsided, I collapsed on top of her. She kissed the side of my face and my ear as I tried to catch my breath.

{ 35 }

I woke up the next morning with the sun peeking between the closed blinds and illuminating the room. As I stretched out, my arm went across the other side and hit nothing but mattress. The revelation was a bit jarring, and so I popped up out of bed to find myself sleeping alone. On the floor, I saw the torn condom wrapper and used condom lying near the bed.

"Why didn't I throw that away?" I muttered to myself.

I picked up the items and went to the bathroom. I threw them in the trash can located between the sink and the toilet. After washing my hands, I made my way back to the bedroom and found only my shorts on the floor. I did a quick scan of the room to see where my shirt was. I couldn't find it so I went into my closet to grab another one.

I got dressed and went downstairs. When I got to the bottom step, I noticed Lisa's dress was folded neatly on the floor with her bra and panties lying on top of the dress. Her shoes were placed next to them. I walked through the hallway into the living room where I saw Lisa sitting on the couch. She was curled up in the middle wearing my T-shirt from last night and with a glass of orange juice sitting on the coffee table in front of her.

"Good morning," I said.

"Morning," she replied as she ran her fingers through her hair. She looked at the juice and then back at me. "Hope you don't mind."

"Nah. You're good." I walked over and sat next to her on the couch. As I laid my arm across the back of it, she scooted over and nuzzled next to me. Her arm was draped across my chest, and her head rested gently on my shoulder.

"How are you feeling?" I asked.

"Wonderful," she whispered. She took a deep breath as she rubbed her hand across my chest. "Man, what a night."

"Yeah," I replied. "What a night." I paused for a moment to wrap my arm around her shoulder and kiss the top of her head. "I saw your clothes in the hallway."

She laughed and said, "I know. I'm such a neat freak. When I woke up and saw my stuff scattered all over the house, I cracked up and started laughing. I though, 'That's not something I'd see at my house.'"

"You were in the throes of passion," I joked. She laughed louder as she patted me on my chest and stomach. "You couldn't get enough of me."

"You know what? I couldn't." She sat up on the couch to where she was level with me. "From the time I left the club, I couldn't stop thinking about you."

"Is that why you asked to come over?"

"That was on a whim. If I hadn't, I probably wouldn't have slept much. You remember when we were dancing and that guy was grinding on me from behind?"

"Oh yeah," I replied. "He was a creepy one, wasn't he?"

"Mr. Casanova," she said sarcastically. "Anyway, when you pulled me away from him and held me close, it felt like everything was right in the world."

"That sounds like a Hallmark moment."

"I'm serious!" she replied. Then she calmed herself down and said, "That was an awesome moment, and I couldn't get it out of my mind. And when you kissed me at the doorway, I was done. Wherever you wanted to take me was fine with me."

I paused and stared at the other side of the room. She then took my hand and clasped it in both of hers, pulling it closer to her chest.

"So are you glad I came over?" she cooed.

"Yes," I replied. "Much better than watching SportsCenter."

She laughed at my last statement, and I wanted to say more but all I could do was laugh with her. Then I leaned in to kiss her. She responded by letting go of my hand and placing one of hers gently at the back of my neck to pull me in closer. Our kisses grew deeper, and I turned slightly to her as my hand grabbed at one of her breasts. I could hear her moan with pleasure with my action. I grabbed it tighter as we continued our lip lock.

"Hold up," she panted as she pulled away.

"What's wrong," I asked.

"Nothing. It's just that I won't make it to brunch with Danny and Alicia if we get started up again." She patted my chest as she smiled at me. "Who can pass up mimosas?"

"Mimosas!" I cheered.

Lisa laughed at my comment as she unwrapped herself from me. "Danny's idea, not mine. But she's my girl, so it's all good." She paused and then said, "You know what Alicia asked me when I was taking them back to Danny's place?"

"What's that?"

"She wanted to know when I was going to fuck you."

I laughed out loud when she told me that. "So what are you going to tell her?"

"Nothing," she playfully replied. Then I looked at her skeptically, figuring there would be some gossip. "Chris, you are too much."

"I'm just saying…"

"I keep my business out of the streets. Look, I better get changed. Where is your bathroom?"

"Down the hall and to the right."

She got up from the couch and made her way to the bathroom. I reached for the remote and turned on the TV. Baseball highlights popped up and the announcers were talking excitedly about a pitcher's flirtation with a no-hitter. Evidently, he made it through seven and a third innings before giving up a double.

"Who are they talking about?" I heard Lisa call out.

"Morris for the Pirates. He almost no-hit the Cubs."

"That stinks. I've got Williams going tonight. Watch him get blasted."

"Works that way, doesn't it?"

She closed the bathroom door, and I continued to watch the sports program. They did a piece on some rookies going through their first pro football minicamp and a free agent signing. Then Lisa walked out wearing her dress from last night as another baseball highlight came on.

"About time Perez hit a home run," she observed. "You know who would go great with..."

"You're not getting Freeman," I cut in with a laugh. When I said that, she playfully threw my T-shirt at me. I picked it up off the coffee table and took a long look at Lisa. She smiled at me as I sat and took in the view.

"You should go to brunch like that," I said.

"Yeah right!" she replied. "I wouldn't hear the end of it from those two."

"Well, that is true."

"I gotta get home and get changed."

I got up from my seat and walked her to the door. As I reached for the doorknob, she gently grabbed my hand.

"I had a great night, Chris," she said.

"Me, too. Why don't you come back when you're done with brunch?"

"Wish I could, but I've got some reports to go over before Monday morning."

"Okay. But let's get together soon."

"Absolutely."

I let go of the doorknob, wrapped my arms around her waist, and gave her a deep kiss. When I let go of her, she had to catch her breath and compose herself before I opened the door to let her out.

{ 36 }

I strolled into work Monday morning with a smile on my face. I waved and nodded to everyone I came across as I made my way to my desk. My team was mingling about in the walkway when I approached.

"Good morning, everybody!" I said.

"Good morning to you," June replied. "Looks like you had a good weekend. It shows all over you."

"I actually did. I ran into some friends of mine, and we went out on the town."

"Good for you," May said. "You deserve to have some fun."

"Well, Monday's here. Let me check in before my meeting with Shelley."

"Have fun with that," Renee joked.

"Tell me about it."

I walked away from the group to my cubicle. I fired up my computer and logged in. After scanning over my notes and my e-mails, I turned to the report I owed Mr. Drake and put on the finishing touches before e-mailing it to him. That's when I heard a knock on the metal partition of my cubicle. I turned around and saw Jennifer standing there.

"You got a minute?" she asked.

"Sure," I replied. "Come on in."

She slipped into my cubicle and leaned against the far desk. "Chris, you've got me curious."

"About what?"

"This morning and that look on your face. I've seen that look before."

"Okay," I said reluctantly. "Where are we going with this?"

"Let's just say my husband's had that same look."

"Your husband?"

"Oh yeah."

"And how..."

"Because I gave him that kind of weekend," she whispered with a devilish grin on her face as her answer caught me by surprise. "What? He's a good man and he deserves it."

"Jennifer," I tried to respond. "I...I...wow."

"So what's her name, big guy?"

"Come on now."

"Chris, you know it won't leave this space."

"Oh goodness," I relented. "Her name is Lisa, and I was with her and her friends this weekend. We danced together all night, and then she ended up at my place."

"Oh my," Jennifer replied. "It was a fun night."

"Yeah, but I felt like we connected. But I always thought that connections were supposed to be different."

"Different? Different how? Chris, there's no checklist or timetable to follow. When it happens, it happens. Trust me."

"Well, you are the married one."

"Let me tell you something," she said as she leaned forward. "Second date with my husband, I knew I was marrying him."

"Wow," I said. "Look, I got to get some stuff done."

"Keep me posted, okay?"

"I will."

Jennifer waved and then left my cubicle. I pondered over what she told me as I started back into the report. That's when I got a buzz from my phone. I pulled it out of my pocket and saw I got a text message from Elle.

Greetings from New York City. My agent booked me for some gigs and recording session up here, even put me up in a studio apartment on Park Avenue. Keep your fingers crossed.

Then I heard a knock behind me. I turned around and saw Shelley there.

"Hey there," she said.

"Hello Shelley," I replied.

"What are you smiling about?"

"Friend of mine is in NYC chasing her dream."

"Oh really," she replied as she slid in my cubicle. "What does she do?"

"Jazz singer. Ever heard of Elle and her Jazz Gents?"

"You know Elle? I saw her at the Carytown Fall Festival last year. She was so good. Now Chris..."

"She's just a friend," I interrupted.

"Chris, she is a gorgeous woman."

"I know, but she's just a friend."

"Okay. I get it," she relented. "But Chris..."

"Take a number," I joked. "You're not the only one who's asking. By the way, I got your e-mail. You wanted to talk to me about something?

"Yes. We've got a job fair coming up at our new store in Chester if you are interested."

"I think I'll pass on this one."

"But you did so well at the Retail Expo last week and..."

"I'm good, but if it's last minute, I may be able to help."

"Sounds like a plan. I'll catch up with you later."

As she left my cubicle, I turned back to my desk to check e-mails. Then I got another buzz from my cell phone. This text was from Laura.

Hey there. I'll be in town for Adult Expo this weekend. How about Friday night...me and you for Round Two? I'm ready to suck you dry again lol.

"Oh yeah," I thought to myself. "Laura's coming to town."

{ 37 }

Lisa and I tried to get together during the week, but she was stuck in meetings after work every night. I went to the gym on Tuesday night and got in a great workout. But going back on Thursday was a whole different episode.

As soon as I walked in, I saw Michelle standing at the front desk in her workout gear. She saw me and then pointed upstairs. There was another woman standing next to her laughing at her antics. She was dressed more business-like, wearing a purple blouse and black slacks. But the thing that stood out about her was the size of her ample chest. It made her nametag, "Melissa", introduce her before she could.

"You!" Michelle called out. "Get dressed and go upstairs."

"No," I cracked back. "Kickboxing is not in the cards. I know what I want to do tonight." Then I turned to Melissa and asked, "Is she always like this?"

She laughed and then replied, "Sometimes. She got me into a couple of classes. Lucky for me tonight, I'm still on the job."

"Yeah, buddy," Michelle jumped in. "She's taken my class. Now it's your turn." She pointed up to the second floor and said, "Let's go."

"Nope," I said as I got my ID scanned by the attendant and started toward the men's locker room. "I'm getting out of here before you get any ideas."

"Hey, hold up," she called out. I turned around, and she caught up with me. "You know I'm messing with you, right?"

"Of course," I replied. "We're supposed to have fun in here."

"Absolutely. But...," she said with a sly smile.

"Oh, will you stop?" I joked. "You are too much."

"I'm going to get you into my class." Then she stepped to the side and wrapped her arm around my waist. "But I'll leave you alone for now."

"Okay," I said as I wrapped my arm around her shoulder. "Have a good class." We gave each other a quick side hug and then she headed upstairs to get ready for her class. Then I saw Melissa approach me.

"Is she always like that with members?" I asked.

"Not all of them," she responded. "Just the ones she thinks are hot." The answer took me by surprise, and I took a step back. She laughed at my response and asked, "You're Chris, right?"

"Yeah," I answered with a bit of hesitation. "How did you know?"

"Your name has come up a couple of times. She's had her eye on you for a while."

"What? Is she stalking me or something?"

"Of course not! Chris, it's a fitness center. People work out here. Don't tell me you haven't noticed anyone you like."

"I haven't exactly been paying attention."

"Yeah, right. You've seen somebody."

"Well, yeah," I relented. "A few."

"So Michelle saw you, too." Then I watched her scan me over. "And I can see why. You're doing a good job taking care of yourself."

"Well, thanks," I answered. "I didn't realize I was commanding that kind of attention."

"Well, you are. Keep it up," she replied as she patted my arm. "Let me finish up some paperwork before I head home. Nice meeting you."

"Nice meeting you, too."

She waved goodbye and went back to her office as I started toward the locker room.

"You got all the women talking to you, huh?" I heard a male voice call out. I looked over to my right, and I saw Tim on one of the stationary bikes.

"Daddy Dearest, what's up?" I said as I approached him. "How's fatherhood?"

"Loving it, man. So what's up with you and the membership lady?"

"Nothing. Just talking about people talking about me."

"Oh shit!" he replied. "Look at you, playboy. Got women checking you out in here? Make that shit happen."

"Look, I'm just trying to do my thing."

"Chris, I get it. Do you thing. It's not like you're talking about a relationship or a marriage. When that shit is ready to happen, it'll happen."

"What are you talking about?"

"Hear me out," he said as he stopped pedaling and got off his bike. He grabbed his water bottle and towel from the bike and made his way to the other side where I was standing. "Don't believe in that fairy tale shit. You think my wife was the only one I was talking to? I was meeting, greeting, hanging out, and fucking as much as I could. When I saw that with my wife was where I wanted to be, I put all the other stuff aside. I had my fun, but I had found myself a home.

"Home?" I replied.

"Yep."

"That simple?"

"Shit yeah," he replied as we started walking toward the stairs. "When it's time, you'll know." He took a peek at the clock on the wall and said, "I need to finish up so I can get home and put the little one to bed. Chris, do your thing. It'll all work out."

"All right, I'll do that."

We gave each other a fist bump, and he went on his way. But after a couple of steps, he turned around and said, "One more thing."

"What's that?"

He whispered, "If you happen to work it out with the one you were talking to, let me know. I just want to know how big her titties are."

"Oh, come on, man!" I responded.

"Hey, hey. I may be a husband and a father, but I'm still a man. If I were single, I'd be all over that just so I could play with what's underneath her blouse."

"Tim, you damn horndog."

He laughed and said, "Always, brother."

{ 38 }

*Hey, Chris. I'm tired as hell from work so I'm calling it a
night. I'll get with you in the morning.*

I missed Lisa's message from having my phone on vibrate
and not picking up on the call. Seeing her message scratched
off the idea of giving her a call. Instead, I went to the grocery
store after work.

When I got home, I put my groceries away and changed
into a T-shirt and shorts. I fired up the PlayStation and
started into a game. That's when my cell phone rang. I picked
it up and saw it was Tony.

"What's going on, man?" I answered.

"Not much," he replied. "What's going on with you?"

"Nothing. Staying in."

"Me, too. I need some rest."

"What's going on?"

"Promotions. We've got some big-time DJs coming to
town to play our events. We're talking Philly, New York,
Atlanta, and one from Miami coming late summer and early
fall."

"Damn, man," I said as I paused my game. "Somebody's
working hard to put Richmond on the map."

"One of the best parts of this merger, man," he replied with pride. "National access. We're sending our local DJs out as well. TNT did some sets in Charlotte last month. Everyone down there said he rocked it."

"Good deal. Glad to hear that."

"So you just staying in?"

"Yep. Me and the PlayStation."

"I heard that. Well, I'm out then."

"Peace."

I hung up the call, placed my cell phone on the coffee table, and resuming playing.

After three games, I decided to shut the system off and watch some TV. The network stations had on reruns, and there wasn't a baseball game on of note. I flipped to some action movie that I didn't recognize but piqued my interest. After a couple of car chase scenes, my cell phone rang. I picked it up and saw it was Laura on the other end.

"Hey, you," I answered.

"Hey, baby," she replied with a slight purr.

"You're in town?"

"Yeah, got in this afternoon. My security guy is with family in New Kent tonight, so I'm free to see you."

"So where are you?" I can pick you up and we can go out and get a drink."

"Don't worry about that. I've got a rental car."

"So where do you want to meet?"

"How about your driveway?" she joked. "I'm parked outside."

"My driveway?" I responded. "How did you…"

"I looked you up. It wasn't too bad of a drive."

"So come to the door."

"Actually…I can't."

"You can't? Why not?"

"Well," she said with a giggle. "There's this woman standing next to me who said I can't come in unless you start taking her kickboxing class."

"Kickboxing?" Then it hit me. "No fucking way!"

I jumped from my seat and ran to the front door. I flung it open and to my astonishment, Laura and Michelle were standing in the driveway arm-in-arm. They had wide smiles on their faces and were waving at me.

"I can't…" I tried to say but I was too much in shock at what I was witnessing. Finally I blurted out, "Get in here!" They laughed and gave each other a high five before skipping their way to the front door.

"Surprise!" Laura cheered as she wrapped her arms tightly around my neck.

"You're not lying," I responded. She let go of me and placed a quick kiss on my lips before walking inside and down the hall. Michelle walked behind her with a sly smile. "So you are a stalker."

"Nah," she replied. "Just having fun with you." She gave me a hug and went inside herself.

"Go on and have a seat," I said as I followed them. They walked over to the couch and sat on each end. "Okay. What do you want? Wine? Beer?"

"You remember what we talked about?" Laura hinted.

"Yes, I do. I got the Merlot and the Zinfandel. I also got a chocolate wine."

"Chocolate?" they both responded.

"Yeah. The guy at the store told me about it. He said some winery in Virginia makes it, and that it's a popular buy. Want me to open it?"

"Go for it," Laura replied.

I headed to the kitchen and pulled out the chocolate wine bottle from the top shelf of the near cabinet.

"So, Chris," Michelle said. "Laura said you two went to high school together."

"John Adams High School," I replied as I pulled out three wine glasses from the cabinet. "Fun times in Northern Virginia."

"That's what she said. Tell me, what was it like to take batting practice in a tutu?"

"Oh God!" I ran back into the living room where I saw both of them smiling at me. "Laura, you told her that story."

"Sorry," she said with a shrug. "I know it was for charity, but you looked so cute in it."

"This is going to be fun," Michelle said with glee. "Chris, pour the wine. Laura, please tell me more."

{ 39 }

Laura spent the next two hours and an entire bottle of wine telling Michelle about our high school days. Hearing the names of our classmates and places we hung out were quite a refreshing recollection. I jumped in with a few details of my own, but Laura had the whole thing under control. Michelle spent more time laughing than she did drinking wine.

"Oh my God," she said out of breath. "You two had a ton of fun."

"High school was interesting," Laura replied. Then she turned to me and raised her glass. "But Chris made it a lot better."

"No problem, lab partner," I said as I raised my glass to her.

"So, Laura," Michelle said. "You told me you were in California."

"Yes," she said as she finished her glass. "I've been out there for a while."

"So what do you do?"

"I'm in the film industry."

"Oooh!" Michelle replied. "That's so cool. So are you an actress?"

"You could say that," Laura answered with a bit of hesitation.

"So what have you been in? Movies? TV?"

"Slow down, Michelle," Laura said. She then reached for the wine bottle and poured the last bit into her glass. "You wouldn't recognize me if you did see me."

"What? I wouldn't...oh. You have a stage name?"

"Yeah, and my movies wouldn't show in your local theater."

"Wait a minute," Michelle said, confused by Laura's answer. "What do you mean by that?"

Laura looked over at me, and I gave her a nod to let the cat out of the bag. She reached for her phone and started tapping the screen. After a few seconds, she found what she was looking for. As she handed the phone to Michelle, she said, "My stage name is Megan Allen."

Michelle took a look at the phone and her face widened in disbelief. With her mouth agape, she looked at Laura and tried to reply but the words couldn't come out. Finally, she broke out in hysterical laughter.

"No fucking way!" she responded. "You're in porn?"

"You got it," Laura replied with a slight laugh.

Michelle looked at me and asked, "Did you know..."

"Found out a few weeks ago," I replied. "Saw her at Paradise Lounge..."

"Wait a minute!" she stopped me. "Megan Allen? At Paradise Lounge?"

"Yes," Laura said. "I was a feature there and..."

"Holy shit! This is too much!" Michelle leaped from her seat and pulled out her phone. She hustled to my seat and shoved it in my hand. "Chris, take our picture!"

"What?" I replied.

"Take our fucking picture!" she said as she sat back down. She scooted next to Laura and put her arm around her shoulder. Laura wasn't sure what was going on but was a good sport about it. She placed an arm around Michelle's shoulder and with the other hand grabbed a firm hold of one of her breasts.

"Whoa," Michelle said in surprise. "You just went right in there."

Laura laughed and said, "I'm guessing this for a bet. So let's make someone jealous."

I took about four pictures of the two women before handing the phone back to Michelle. "So what's going on?"

"Chad," she replied. "Personal trainer? Short guy with dreads?"

"Yeah, I know who you're talking about."

"Anyway, he and some of the guys were supposed to go to Paradise Lounge for his bachelor party. They took up a pool and bet to see who was going to get their picture taken with Megan first."

"Well, I didn't see any guy with dreads or any long hair," Laura said.

"That's because his fiancée got wind of their plans." Michelle then reached out and gently laid her hand on Laura's wrist. "I heard she went the fuck off on him. She threatened to call off the wedding if he went."

"That's fucked up," I said. "I take it he obliged and the pool money never got dished back out."

"It's still in an envelope in Chad's desk...until our meeting Sunday morning."

"You go, girl!" Laura cheered as she gave Michelle a high five. "But too bad for Chad. I was only there to dance and entertain the crowd. It's not like I'm trying to fuck the customers."

I snickered at her comment, causing her to look my way.

"Wait a minute," Michelle said. "What's going on?"

"What do you mean?" Laura replied.

"I saw the way you looked at him," she teased. "Spill it, girl."

"Yeah, Laura," I joked. "What's up?"

"You stop it," she playfully scolded as she shook her index finger at me. "You're not innocent in this either." Then she turned to Michelle and said, "This stays here."

"Absolutely."

Then Laura motioned for Michelle to lean in. She whispered something in her ear, causing Michelle to back away with a surprised look on her face.

"Shut up," she quietly said. She turned to me with a wide grin on her face. Then Laura tapped her on the shoulder to get her to lean in again. She whispered something else but this time Michelle had a look of amazement on her face. She pointed at me and Laura nodded her head in approval.

"Time out," I said. "What's going on over there?"

"Girl talk," they chimed in at the same time.

"Come on. You're in my house…"

"We don't care," Michelle said. "This is between us."

"What she said," Laura added. Then she got up and asked, "Restroom?"

"Down the hall and to the right," I directed. As she walked past me, I looked at Michelle. She looked back with a playful look of defiance. When Laura closed the bathroom door, I pointed back and forth between her and Michelle. Sensing an inquiry, Michelle smiled and nodded her head no.

"Come on," I mouthed to her silently.

"No," she mouthed back.

I left my seat and sat next to her on the couch. I leaned in and whispered, "Tell me."

Michelle smiled back at me as she nodded in disapproval. I moved in closer and placed my hand at the back of her neck.

"What are you doing?" she playfully whispered.

"Tell me what she said," I answered.

"I don't think so."

We stared at each other, and then I watched her tongue dart across her upper lip. That's when I took a deep breath and made a move, pressing my lips against hers. It caught her by surprise, but she quickly fell into the moment and kissed me back.

Then I heard the flush of the bathroom toilet and the opening of the door. I quickly turned my attention toward the direction of the noise. That's when Michelle grabbed my wrist and turned me over to where my back was squarely planted on the couch. She climbed on top of me and straddled me on the couch. I could feel my erection bulging from my shorts and rubbing in between her legs. She leaned in and kissed me again.

"Oh man," I heard Laura say as she entered the room. "I wanted to get on top of him first."

"I guess I beat you to him," Michelle replied as Laura took a seat at the edge of the couch. "And you're right."

"Told you."

"Told her what?" I asked.

Laura crawled over to us and whispered in my ear, "That you got a big one, baby." She then licked all around my earlobe as Michelle kissed down the other side of my neck. I let out a deep breath as the sensation of two mouths on me felt amazing. "Have fun with her. Right now I wanna watch." Laura slid back to the edge of the couch and curled up in her seat. She winked at me as Michelle grabbed my face.

She held it in her hands and kissed me again. My arms were wrapped around her, and my hands made their way under her shirt. I could feel the tautness in her back muscles and her shoulders as her arms moved to drape themselves over my head. As I felt her sports bra, Michelle leaned away from me and smiled. She then took off her shirt, showing a bright yellow sports bra and her six-pack abs.

"Man, you're ripped," I said as I ran my fingers across her stomach.

"Damn right," she proudly replied. "I worked my ass off for this body."

Then she pointed over to where Laura was sitting. I saw she had a hand underneath her undone shorts and was pleasuring herself. She glanced at us for a moment and then she closed her eyes, sinking deeper into her own wares.

I tugged upward on Michelle's bra and over her head, revealing two pierced nipples staring at me. "When did you do this?" I asked as I gently played with them.

"About six months ago," she answered. Then she closed her eyes and tilted her head back. She moaned, "That feels good. You have nice hands."

"Thanks. It helps to have something nice to play with."

"Listen to you." Michelle tugged at my shirt, and I helped her take it off, exposing my naked chest. She ran her hands across it before resting them on top of my shoulders. "I like what I see, too." Then she leaned down and took a nipple into her mouth. The sensation of her sucking, licking, and biting it almost too my breath away. I moaned out loud as I threw my head back against the couch.

Then I felt a slight tap on my chest. I looked up and saw Laura had made her way over to me. She looked at Michelle and purred, "I want some of him." Michelle moved over and each took a side of my chest and started kissing it. I tried to look at their handiwork, but all I could do was close my eyes and take it all in.

My eyes popped open as I felt a hand grab my crotch. I looked and saw Michelle had a firm grip on my erection, squeezing me through my shorts. Laura made her way upward and was kissing me as Michelle worked her hand inside my shorts and started stroking me.

"You are so hard," she said. "I need this in my mouth." She pulled off my shorts and moved in between my thighs.

"Look at you," Laura said.

"Hey, I like being on my knees." Then she took the head of my dick into her mouth and sucked it.

"Feel good, baby?" Laura whispered in my ear. I nodded my head in approval as Michelle took me deeper in her mouth. Laura took off her shirt and bra and put one of her breasts in my mouth.

"Oh fuck," I moaned.

"You wanna fuck?" Laura cooed. I nodded as I placed my hand on the back of Michelle's head to push her mouth further down on me. Laura whispered, "Nuh uh. Not yet." Then she slid away from me and off the couch. She crawled in between my legs and next to Michelle.

"What are you doing?" Michelle asked her.

"Gotta take care of the boys," Laura said.

"The boys?"

"Watch." She leaned down and took one of balls in her mouth. Michelle gasped for a second as Laura continued to suck slowly. The sensation of Laura's mouth and Michelle's hand stroking made me moan louder than before.

"Oh, you like that," Michelle whispered to me before taking me back in her mouth.

I watched them for a bit take turns alternating between dick and balls. Then I reached for both of their heads and pulled them away from my crotch. I kissed each deeply before saying, "I wanna fuck both of you."

"Both of us?" Michelle replied. "You got what it takes?"

"Oh yeah." Then I looked at Laura and mouthed quietly to her, "Round two."

She nodded in approval and then asked, "Where do you want us, baby?"

"Upstairs," I instructed. "Let's go to my bedroom."

{ 40 }

I woke up around nine thirty in the morning relaxed but drained. Fucking Laura and Michelle turned into a marathon sex session. Swimming through two bodies was quite an experience. There weren't too many points in the action where my dick wasn't in someone's mouth or pussy as the orgasms between the three of us piled up.

I looked to either side of me and found a naked female body snuggled under my arm. Each had their hand resting softly on my chest, rising and falling with each of my breaths. I looked upward at the pale white ceiling and stared at it for a while. I finally let out a quiet laugh, marveling at the position I was in.

Then I felt an index finger tilt my head to the right. I looked and saw Michelle smiling at me.

"What are you laughing at?" she whispered.

"I can't believe this happened."

She gently kissed me on the lips and cooed, "It did, baby. Crazy, isn't it?"

"Yeah. How do you feel?"

"Amazing. It's been a while since I've come that hard."

"What are you two talking about?" Laura asked as she peered over my shoulder. She wiped her hair from her face while trying to open her sleepy eyes.

"Last night," I said. "Someone over here came like crazy."

"Me too," she purred as she rested her head on my chest. She kissed me and said, "You were amazing." Then she looked over at Michelle. "And so were you." She leaned over me, gently grabbed her by her head, and kissed her.

"It's been a while for that, too," Michelle replied.

"Being with another woman?"

"Yeah. It's a long story." Michelle nuzzled her head back in my chest and asked, "What time is it?"

"About nine thirty," I groaned.

"Mmmm. That's nice."

"Hey, Laura. What time do you have to be at the expo?"

"Not until three," she said as she gently brushed the back of my hand on my cheek. "Why? Wanna go again?"

"No," I replied as I sunk back into the pillow. "I'm drained."

"Well, I hope you're not too drained to make some breakfast."

"Breakfast?"

"Yeah," Michelle jumped in. "Make us breakfast."

"Breakfast," I groaned. "What do you want?"

"Surprise us."

"Okay," I said as I rose up in a seated position. "You two are lucky I picked up groceries last night."

"Goodie," Laura cheered. "Have fun in the kitchen, baby."

I crawled over her and put my feet on the floor. After taking a quick stretch, I lumbered out of the bedroom and headed downstairs. I got to the living room and found out clothes crumpled all over the floor. I found my shorts and shirt near the couch and put them both on before entering the kitchen.

But then I had the impulse to turn around and find my phone sitting on the coffee table. I picked it up and checked the screen. I saw that Lisa had called me earlier in the morning. I placed the phone on the kitchen counter and played her message, and I went searching through the fridge.

Hey. Sorry I didn't get with you last night. I just needed to get away from everyone. Hope you're doing fine.

"Oh, I'm doing fine," I said to myself as I took the eggs and milk out of the fridge.

I was hoping to catch up with you at the gym this morning. Anyway, maybe you and I can go do something today. Give me a call when you get a chance. Take care.

"How many women you got, big boy?"

The voice caught me by surprise. I turned around and found Laura at the kitchen opening, wearing only a smile on her face.

"How long have you been standing there?" I asked.

"Long enough."

"Where's Michelle?"

"Wiped out," she responded as she went back to the living room to find her clothes. "Too bad."

"Too bad?" I replied as I pulled out a mixing bowl. "Oh, let me guess. You wanted to play with her again while I was down here making breakfast."

"Chris, she is hot. Do you blame me?"

"Yeah, but...last night was crazy."

"Never had a threesome before?"

"Nope," I said as I took out some batter from the top shelf.

"Well," she said as she finished tidying up the last bit of her clothes. "You were up to the challenge." She came into the kitchen and took a seat on the counter. "So who's on the phone?"

"Oh, no one."

"Come on, Chris. There's no way you'd have your phone on the counter if there wasn't someone leaving you a message you wanted to hear." I turned away from her and kept working on breakfast. "Who is it?"

"Nobody."

"Bullshit. Give me a name." Then she grabbed my phone and started tapping on the screen.

"What are you doing?" I inquired forcefully. "Will you give me that?"

"Lisa," she said playfully as she looked at my screen. "Oh, that's funny. She called you this morning while we were in bed."

"Come on, Laura," I pleaded. "Stop it, okay?"

"Stop what?" Then she paused as she hopped down off the counter. "You like her, don't you?" I shrugged and continued with putting together the ingredients. "Chris, talk to me."

"Laura...okay, I like her," I replied. "She's fun as hell to be with. She's tough, but she does have a tender side. But..."

"Chris, I get it. Look, you and I will always be friends, great sex or no sex. No matter what, I'll stand by you." She wrapped her arm around my waist and gave it a firm squeeze. "But if she's like one of the Franklin sisters..."

"Goodness, don't mention them." I started to laugh as I took a pan out of the bottom cabinet near the stove. As I placed it on the stove eye, I grabbed the oil from the top counter and turned the heat up on the pan. "She's nothing like them."

"Better not be. But seriously, it sounds like you're curious to see where this goes." She glanced upward and then back at me. "Michelle, that's probably a one-night fling. But I bet she'll send you some referral pussy."

"Referral pussy?" I asked as I continued to mix the batter. "What the fuck is that?"

"She's gonna tell one of her friends how well you fucked her, and that friend's gonna want to fuck you."

"Sounds like you've done some referring before," I joked. She shrugged and made a not-so innocent look on her face.

"But enough about that," Laura said. "Give Lisa a call."

"I will," I replied.

"Right now."

"What? You and Michelle are here."

"Michelle's still upstairs, and I'll be quiet. I'll chop up some fruit while you cook pancakes and talk to her."

"Yeah right."

"Just call her," she insisted while digging into my fridge. She found a quart of strawberries and blueberries in the fridge and a package of bacon. "And put her on speakerphone, too."

"Oh, hell no," I replied. "Now I know you're crazy. Listening in on my conversation?"

"What are you two talking about?" Michelle asked as she made her way to the kitchen opening.

"Pancakes," I responded.

She laughed as she went into the living room to put her clothes on. "And today's not a cheat day. Oh well, I'll have to pay for it later. What else are you gonna put in there?"

"I don't know. Laura took out some blueberries and strawberries.

"Oooh!" she said. "Strawberries and blueberries! Put those in there."

"In where?"

"In the batter."

"Oh, I see where you're going." I looked at Laura and she smiled at me. "Laura, cut those up and throw them in the batter. This ought to be interesting."

{ 41 }

After breakfast, Laura and Michelle left, and I sat in the kitchen staring at a mound of dishes. I had no intention of standing at the sink and washing all of them, so I put everything in the dishwasher. Just as I was about to grab the detergent from underneath the sink, I glanced at my phone still sitting on the counter. I grabbed it and dialed up Lisa.

"Hey," she said as she picked up immediately.

"Hey there," I replied. "How are you? Feel better after getting away from everyone?"

"Absolutely. I needed the rest. What about you? I hope you didn't go to bed early or anything?"

I laughed to myself at her comment. "Of course not."

"I should've been over there with you."

Knowing what had transpired in my house, the comment caught me by surprise. "I...I thought you wanted to get away from everyone."

"I did," she sighed. "But you were on my mind all night."

"Really?" I answered slowly. "Wow."

"Chris, ever since the club and at your place...I feel differently about you."

"Different? Different how?"

"You're not just a guy to me anymore. I know we hang out at the gym, and I talk about kicking you ass in fantasy league."

"Kicking my ass?" I joked. "That's not happening."

"Chris," she pleaded. "Let's be serious for once. No sports."

"Whoa," I replied. "Okay. What's really going on?"

She paused for a couple of moments and then blurted out, "Chris, I really like you." She took a couple of deep breaths before continuing. "That night at the club...I swear when you danced with me, I felt this connection with you and..."

"Hold on, Lisa," I butted in. "That sounds nice and..."

"Oh, I get it. You're seeing someone else."

"No!" I shouted. "I'm not seeing anyone."

"What? You don't like me?"

"No!" I calmed myself down and sunk back in my seat. "It's none of that, Lisa. I just...I didn't see this coming. I'm flattered that you thought about me."

"Well, thanks. So what's next?"

"How about a date?"

"A date?"

"Yes. Let's go on a date. Nothing where we have to get all dressed up or anything. I can pick you up and we can go out to Deep Run Park, you and me walking around, and maybe watch the ducks swim in the lake."

"That doesn't sound like a date to me," she joked.

"What do you suggest? Watching golf on TV?"

"That is true," she replied. "There is nothing on. So... when are we going to have this 'date'?"

"In an hour. I just need to shower and get dressed. Where do you live?"

"You know where Braxton Village is?"

"Off of Three Chopt? Yeah, I know where that is."

"Fifteen hundred D."

"Cool. I'll see you in a bit."

"Okay. See ya."

I hung up the phone and took a deep breath. I quickly got up from my seat and headed back to the kitchen. I finished loading up the dishwasher and then wiped off the counters. Then I headed upstairs to get a shower and get dressed.

Blue skies and very few clouds hovered over me as I drove to Lisa's place. I put on my shades and leaned back in the seat as the hard thumping beats from the radio made me relax. I drove with a single hand on top of the steering wheel and my head nodding to the music. I reached Lisa's complex and drove slowly down the main street until I got to her building.

As soon as I got to the sidewalk, Lisa popped out of her apartment. She quickly approached me and wrapped her arms tightly around my waist. I draped my arm around her shoulders and leaned in to kiss her. She gladly responded, and we stayed locked together for a while.

"Good to see you," she replied.

"You too. Ready?"

"Yeah. Let's go." She clasped her hand in mine, and we walked over to the passenger side door. I opened it to let her in, and then I got in on my side.

"You know," she said. "I could get used to this."

"Get used to what?" I asked.

"You and I just being together and doing next to nothing."

"We're going to the park," I said as I turned on the ignition. "It isn't exactly next to nothing." I pulled out of the space and started heading out of the complex. "But I get what you're saying. And I feel the same way."

{ 42 }

I didn't get back to the gym until Thursday night. I got into my workout by riding the stationary bike for about thirty minutes. Then I headed upstairs to the weight area. Once I got situated on the bicep curl station, I felt a fist gently tap my shoulder. I took my headphones off and saw Michelle standing by my side.

"What are you up to?" I asked.

"About to start class," she replied. "Hint, hint."

"I'll be in there eventually."

"I've heard that line before," she responded as she crossed her arms.

"I'll get there."

"You better."

"So, how are you? Recover from the other night?"

She tilted her head back and laughed out loud. Then she uncrossed her arms and leaned forward on the weight section of the machine. "You and Laura wore me out. I wasn't really straight until Monday."

"Good thing or bad thing?" I replied quietly with a sly smile on my face.

Sensing the edge of my question, Michelle smiled back at me. "Actually, I really needed that." She then looked up at the clock of one of the TV screens. "Class calls. But we do need to talk more."

"About what?"

"What do you think, big guy?" she replied as tapped my arm. "Talk to you later." She darted off, and I went back to working out.

As I was moving to the next station, I happened to catch Melissa walk by me. She was giving a tour of the location to a young couple and their two kids. Her attention wandered to me, and she waved with a wide smile on her face. Then she mouthed to me, "We need to talk."

Her words caught me by surprise, and I looked back with skepticism. I pointed to myself in a questionable manner, and she nodded yes. I gave her a thumbs-up and continued with my workout.

After finishing up, I went back to the locker room to change. I was walking toward the exit when I looked over at the offices on the left and saw Melissa sitting in the middle one working on paperwork. I took a detour and made my way to her.

"Hey," I said as I knocked on the door. "What's up?"

"Hey you," she replied cheerfully. "Come on in." I took a seat inside her office and then she said, "Close the door."

The words made me pause as I wondered what she had in mind. As I closed the door, I watched her lean slightly over her desk with a devilish grin on her face.

"I'll just cut to the chase," she said. "I heard you and your friend fucked the shit out of Michelle."

"Oh, come on," I groaned.

"Hey, hey, hey," she responded. "Michelle's my girl, and it's only between us. No gossip here. That's for other people." Then she leaned back in her chair and laughed. "But we are going for a nice lunch with the money she won from the pool."

"The pool?" I questioned. Then what she was talking about hit me. "Oh that."

"Oh yeah. So you and her were high school classmates? That's nuts."

"Yeah. It's wild, but..." My voice trailed off and I tucked my head inward. Then I looked up at her and asked, "And you're not gonna tell anyone?"

"Of course not," she assured me. "The guys only know Michelle met her at random and I know she won't tell them about hooking up with her. Anyway, there is something I want to ask you."

"What's that?" I slowly asked her.

"Can I get a turn?" she cooed.

"A turn?"

"Yeah. I want to see what Michelle was talking about. And Chris?"

"What?"

"I like to be on my knees, too," she whispered with a smile.

Her words caused an instant bulge in my pants. The erection was quite discomforting, and I had to adjust my seating position to relieve the tension.

"Wow," I replied. "I didn't see that coming. Are you always that forward?"

"I can be. So?"

"So what?"

"Can I get a turn?"

Then my phone buzzed in my pocket. I took it out and saw that Lisa was calling me. For a moment I thought about answering it. But as I looked back at Melissa, I thought against it.

"What are you doing tonight?" I asked.

"Nothing I can't cancel."

"What time are you done here?"

"Thirty minutes, tops."

I took a deep breath and said, "Come to my house when you're done."

{ 43 }

Forty-six minutes after I walked out of Melissa's office, she was naked in my bedroom and showing me just how much she liked being on her knees. She gave quite a spirited blowjob and could easily take all of me in her mouth. As she continued, I looked up at my reflection in the mirror. Watching her head bob back and forth put quite a smile on my face, and I couldn't help but give myself a thumbs-up in the mirror.

I reached to her face and gave her a long kiss. "I wanna fuck you."

"Yes, baby," she purred. "Fuck me from behind."

"Get on the bed."

She got up and crawled on the bed. I grabbed a condom from the bathroom closet and quickly slipped it on. I got ready to go inside her when the doorbell rang.

"Who is that?" she asked.

"Don't worry about it," I said as I entered her.

"Oooh," she moaned. "That feels good."

As I started up, the doorbell rang again.

"Oh, forget them, baby," she purred. "You keep fucking me."

"I'm not going anywhere," I replied.

"Good. Now pull my hair."

"Do what?"

"Pull my hair," she panted. "I love it when a guy does that."

I shook my head in disbelief but I did what she asked for. I reached out and grabbed a handful of her hair and pulled her head back. I put my other hand on her shoulder and picked up my pace.

"Fuck yeah!" she moaned. "Fuck me, baby."

The sex got hot and heavy, and I felt sweat forming on my brow. Beads of sweat were forming on Melissa's back, and her hair was starting to get matted. I still had a hold of her hair when she started to pull away from me. I let go of her, and she collapsed on my bed. She turned over and tried to catch her breath.

"Oh my God," she panted. "You are something else."

I grabbed her by the ankles and spread her legs apart. "You ready to keep going?"

"No," she begged. "Give me a minute. I'll get you hard again when I'm ready."

I crawled over to the other side of the bed and lay next to her. I kissed her while I let my hand rub across her breasts.

"I see you like the twins," she said. She closed her eyes and settled her head deep in my pillow. "That feels so good."

"These are nice to play with," I replied.

"All the better to finish off on."

"Oh, so that's where you want me to come. I need to fuck you more before that can happen."

"Oh no. I wanna rest."

"No way," I said I got back up. I moved back in between her legs and entered her once more. I started to pump away and watching the way her breasts bounced up and down with each stroke made me want to pick up the pace. The faster and more forceful I fucked her, the more her breasts bounced and the louder her moans echoed through the bedroom.

When I was about to reach orgasm, I took myself out of her, took off the condom, and straddled her body, my dick inches from her tits.

"Shoot it right here, baby," she purred as she squeezed her breasts together. After a few strokes, I fired off several streams across her chest and one shooting past it and landing on her chin.

"Wow," she said. "That was so good, baby." I collapsed by her and paused to catch my breath. She leaned over and kissed me. "Michelle was right. You're awesome."

"Thanks," I said.

We rested on the bed for a few minutes, my arm over her shoulder and her resting by my head. Then she got up and went to the bathroom. As I heard the water run in the sink, I could also hear the faint sounds of my cell phone ringing. I decided to leave it be and sprawled myself out on the bed.

Melissa came back from the bathroom and crawled on top of me. She reached down, placed her hands on my face, and kissed me. Then I wrapped my arms around her and squeezed.

"I can't stay," she whispered. "I've got to be in the gym at six tomorrow."

"Six in the morning?" I groaned. "Too damn early."

"Best time to work out," she replied as she crawled off me. "Then I can get a shower, and I'm ready for work."

She started to put her panties on. I got out of bed and fumbled around for my clothes. But I had to get one last grab of her breasts. I reached out and latched on to each one as she stood up with her bra in her hand.

"I wanted to fall asleep on these," I joked.

"You're not the first guy to say that," she replied with a laugh. "But I really need to go." She put her bra on and got herself fixed up in the mirror. "Maybe next time."

"I'll remember that."

We got dressed and headed downstairs. As I reached for the door, I paused and took a look at Melissa. "I'm curious. What are you going to say to Michelle?"

"We'll compare notes," she replied. "Then give each other a high five." I shook my head in amazement and laughed. "Don't worry. Your secret's safe with us." She pulled me away from the door, wrapped her arms around my neck, and kissed me deeply. I wrapped my arms around her waist and then my hands ventured downward and squeezed her butt, causing her to slightly gasp as our lips locked.

"Look at you," she replied as we let go of each other. "Trying to get started again?"

"I wouldn't mind you on your knees again," I said with a sly smile.

She laughed and said, "You know what. I do need to go. Sleep tight." She gave me a kiss, and I let her out. When I closed the door, I leaned against it and gave myself a couple of fist bumps.

I walked triumphantly through the hallway and to the living room. As I took a seat on the La-z-boy, I turned on the TV to catch the latest sports highlights. After watching the Braves get another victory, I got up and made my way back to my bedroom. My cell phone was sitting on the dresser, and I flipped it on to check messages. There was a text from Lisa. When I read it, my joyous and celebratory mood quickly soured.

You asshole.

"Oh shit."

{ 44 }

I didn't call Lisa that night.

I didn't call Lisa the next night, either.

On Saturday morning, I got to the gym right when they opened at seven. I changed into my workout clothes and headed out. As I was filling my water bottle, I saw a guy walk into the doorway for the basketball courts. When he opened the door, I could see a female inside taking a shot. My curiosity got the best of me, and I headed that way. When I looked in the window, I saw Lisa shooting by herself.

I walked in and said, "Hey."

She nodded and set up for another shot. I placed my towel and water bottle down at the base of the wall. When I picked my head up, I was shocked to see the basketball was fired straight at my head. Just in the nick of time, I fell back and scrambled away as the ball made a sickening thud to the concrete wall.

"What the fuck, man?" I yelled.

"Who the fuck was that in your house?" she growled.

"What are you talking about?"

"The other night," she replied as she picked up the ball as it rolled back to her.

"The other night?"

"Yeah, asshole," she barked as she threw the ball at me again.

This time I was ready and I caught it. That's when I realized she was at the door when I was with Melissa. "That was you, wasn't it? You were at the door."

"Damn right it was."

As I took a couple of dribbles, Lisa charged after me and aggressively tried to steal the ball away. I turned to my side to shield her, and all she could do was reach for air. Then she fired an elbow into my side. I flinched, and she got around me to steal the ball.

"What the hell was that for?" I snapped.

"For being a jerk," she cracked back as she tried to cross me over. I stepped the wrong way, and she drove by me for a layup.

"So are you spying on me now?" I asked as she briskly walked past me to the top of the key.

"No! I wanted to see you."

"You should've called first."

"Oh," she said as she fired the ball back at me. "You want to keep your women in check?"

"Lisa, no!" I replied as I checked the ball back to her. "It's not even like that."

"Then what is it?" she said.

She took a shot from outside the three-point line, and it clanged off the back of the rim. I charged after the rebound with Lisa right next to me. I stuck my hip out to keep her away from the ball. She took a step to the side but quickly stepped up to defend me. I backed her down to the lane area with her putting up more and more resistance as I got closer to the basket. But then I dropped my shoulder and charged toward the hoop, knocking her down in the process.

After I made the basket, I turned to Lisa and said, "What do you want from me?" I offered a hand to help her up but she slapped it away and got up on her own.

"You can't see it, can you?" she huffed.

"See what?"

"I like you," she replied, poking me in the chest with each word. "I like being around you. But I don't want to me part of some damn rotation, someone to call when you're bored and horny."

"No!" I screamed. "You're crazy." I walked away from her and back to the top of the key."

"Am I?" she snarled. "You called her up, didn't you?"

"None of your business," I replied as I checked the ball to her. She held it for a moment and fired it back at me.

I looked up, and I saw Lisa drop her head in her chest. I took a dribble and then picked it up. I stood and watched her rise up and show her face to me. Her bottom lip was quivering, and there was a tear in each eye.

"I let my guard down for this?" she said quietly. "I thought we connected?"

"We did," I replied.

"But Chris, where did I go wrong? I want a chance with you, not some competition with other women you're banging on the side. I don't want to compete. I just want you. If

I can't have that, then let me go." She wiped the tears away with her sleeve of her T-shirt as I looked up at the ceiling and took a deep breath.

"Chris," she said. "Was it worth it killing the nice guy in you for all of this?"

The question felt like a shot to the heart. I staggered a couple of steps before dropping the ball. It slowly bounced toward Lisa and she picked it up. She offered to check the ball back to me, but I meekly nodded no.

{ 45 }

I spent a full month away from the gym. My life was a straight path from home to work and back. Lisa's last question lingered in my mind, and I just didn't have the ability to shake it. A.J. and Tony tried to get me out to Top Of The World, but I would always make up an excuse to not go. I didn't call any of the women in my phone, and I left Lisa alone, figuring I needed to clear my head.

One day at work, I got a knock on my cubicle side. I turned around and saw April standing in the opening.

"We're having a meeting," she stated.

"A meeting?" I asked. I looked back at my calendar on my computer and said, "I don't see anything..."

"It's not. Just come to the conference room."

I got up from my seat and went over to the conference room. When I got there, my team was seated all around the table. April closed the door behind me, and we took up the remaining seats at the table.

"Okay," I said. "What's going on?"

"Chris," Renee began. "First of all, whatever's going on, thank you for not taking it out on us."

"But what is going on, Chris?" May asked. "You have been moping around this office for a while, and we're concerned."

"Chris, you look like you're searching for something, and it's killing you that you can't find it," James added.

"Geez," I replied. "Have I looked that bad?"

"Oh yeah," Jennifer replied. "Chris, you're an awesome guy and a great leader. We do better when you're happy and engaged. It just hasn't been the same lately. So what's up?"

"I'm glad you're concerned," I said. "But it's something I've got to figure out myself."

"Talk to us."

"Trust me on this on. You'll know when I get it straight."

"You better," June replied.

"I will. Is there anything else?"

"I'm off next week," James said. "Did you get my Day-force entry?"

"Yes, and I've got it noted. Anyone else?"

Then there was a knock on the door. I got up and opened it to find Mr. Drake standing there.

"Chris," he said. "I didn't realize you guys were having a meeting."

"Impromptu and real quick. Couple of things we needed to go over. Are we good, guys?"

A chorus of "Yes" chimed amongst my team. They got up from their chairs as I walked with Mr. Drake to my cubicle.

"How can I help you?" I asked.

"Your report was excellent," he replied. "It was exactly what I was looking for. Look, I know this is extremely short notice, but I want you to go to Philadelphia tonight and meet with the regional team in the morning about what you put together."

"Tonight?" I replied in surprise. "That is quick notice."

"Can you do it?"

"Yes, sir. What do I need to do?"

"Nothing. I'll get everything arranged for you. Hotel, directions to their office, who you'll meet, and the agenda. You just go home and get packed."

"I will, Mr. Drake."

"And besides," he replied as he leaned in. "You could use some time out of the office. I can tell something's bugging you. Maybe a change of scenery will clear your head."

"Have I been that bad?" I asked.

"You have."

"I'm sorry."

"Don't be. Life does that to all of us."

"How soon will I get everything?"

"I can give you what you need in about fifteen minutes. If I were you, I'd get out of here early enough so you don't get caught in DC traffic."

"Got it," I said. "I'll pack up here as soon as I get it."

"Sounds like a plan. Report back to me when you get back in town, okay?"

"Will do."

"Good deal." Mr. Drake left my area, and I immediately went to my team's cubicles.

"Hey guys, poke your heads out for a sec," I said. "I need to go over a few things."

I was on the road to Philly by three that afternoon. Traffic going through wasn't too bad as I got through DC and Baltimore without too many headaches. After I went through the Baltimore Tunnel, I decided to give Damon a call. I dialed his number and put him on speakerphone.

"What's up, man?" he answered.

"Heading your way!" I replied.

"To Philly?"

"Last minute plans. Boss wants me to meet with our regional team there. Told me this morning I had to pack and come up."

"How long are you in town?"

"One night. Tomorrow I got my meetings and then it's back to Richmond."

"Damn. I would get with you, but Angela and I are going to a gala at the Art Museum."

"Wow. Aren't you getting fancy?"

"Dude, you have no idea." He paused for a moment and said, "Angela's doing it big up here, and you know how I do. Look, we were just in the *Philadelphia Daily News*."

"Get the fuck out of here!" I replied.

"No shit," he cracked back. "I'll e-mail you the article."

"Damn," I said. "So y'all going strong?"

"Damn right."

"Let me ask you something, man. How did you know?"

"Know what?"

"How did you know she was it? That she was the place you needed to be?"

"Chris, I used to be fucked up when I had to leave Richmond and come home," he answered. "That's when I knew. You're my brother from another mother, and I love you. But I kept coming down to Richmond because I couldn't get enough of her."

"For real? That's deep."

"You have no idea. When she finally agreed to come up here, you wouldn't believe how much relief I felt. Now I wake up every morning, and it's all good."

"I feel you. But let me ask you this."

"Go ahead."

Traffic stalled for a moment for an accident on the shoulder but quickly dispersed. "Remember when we did that exercise at my house? You wanted me to write down 'I'm a nice guy' and rip it up?"

"Yeah. It worked for you, right?"

"You have no idea."

"Like what?"

"A threesome."

"What!" he screamed. "I could never pull that shit off. How the fuck, man?"

"Well, my friend from high school Laura..."

"Is that the porn chick?"

"My friend from high school Laura," I replied in a huff. "She was in town for an expo, and then one of the girls from gym happened to stop by at the same time."

"Look at you! Work it out!"

"Then that girl told one of her friends…"

"Wait a minute!" he cut in. "Are you telling me you got referral pussy after the threesome?"

"Damon…"

"You did! Wow! I gotta tell the guys…"

"No!" I said. "Damon, stop it. Look, I need to know this. Did I kill the 'nice guy' in me?"

"Didn't you want to kill him?" he replied. "Isn't that what you wanted?"

"But at what price?"

"Oh," he said. "I get it now. There's someone else, isn't it? Somebody you really like?"

"Yeah, there is. But I think I fucked it up with her." For a few moments, there was only the sound of my tires rolling on the interstate. Finally, I asked, "What do I do?"

"Chris," Damon replied. "You never 'killed' the 'nice guy'. You can't. It's just in your DNA. You just moved him to the side. It sounds to me like you need to bring him back, and he'll take you where you need to be."

"I don't know, man. It might be too late."

"Fuck that shit. It's never too late. If she really likes you, she'll let you back in. Is this where you want to be?"

"You know what?" I replied. "The more I drive, the more I believe it is."

"Then bring him back," Damon said. "Hey, I need to get ready. Too bad I'm not free to see you."

"You got better plans that me, man. Have fun at the gala, and tell Angela I said hello."

"I will. Handle your business, man."

"You know me." I paused and then said, "Peace."

{ 47 }

I arrived at the Embassy Suites hotel and parked near the back of the lot. I rolled my luggage behind me and made my way inside to the front desk.

"Good evening, sir," the female attendant said. "How may I help you?"

"Reservation for Chris Wheeler," I replied.

"Yes, sir," she said as she searched her computer. "May I see your ID, please?"

I took out my wallet and showed her my driver's license. I looked over at the plaza, and I saw a group of men gathered around with drinks in their hand.

"Is that a bar over there in the plaza?" I asked as I turned back to the attendant.

"Yes it is. We have a complimentary Happy Hour from four to seven thirty." Then she handed me back my license. "We've got you set up. I just need to make your key." She took out an electronic card and scanned it in her computer. Then she placed it in a sleeve and handed it to me. "Your room number is three eighteen. Have a good stay."

"Thank you," I replied.

I rolled my luggage to the elevator and hit the button to go up. An older man walked beside me and waited just like

I did. I looked back at the plaza and saw a brief commotion of guys taking their picture with a woman wearing a purple dress and black heels. There was a larger man trying to keep things organized and orderly.

"What's going on over there?" I asked the man.

"Some chick in adult films is staying here, and those young bucks are losing their shit," he said with a chuckle. "You would've thought they saw Miss America. Jesus Christ."

"Sounds like you're not into that," I said as the elevator opened.

"Man, I've seen enough *Playboy* and *Penthouse* magazines to fill a library," he said as we got in. "But when you got good lovin' at home, you don't need to see any of that. Your porn star is at home, if you know what I mean. You married?"

"No," I replied.

"Seeing anybody?"

"I may be. That's what I'm trying to figure out," I said as the elevator stopped on the third floor.

As we got off, the man said, "Let me give you a bit of advice. When you're single, there's nothing wrong with playing the field. But when love smacks your ass upside the head, you better stop and listen. It's trying to tell you where you need to be. Otherwise, you'll be chasing forever, and you'll end up old, bitter, and alone."

"Thanks. I'll remember that."

"Looks like you're here on business," he said, pointing at my luggage.

"Regional meeting," I replied.

"Knock 'em dead," he replied with a smile. He went on his way and I started toward my room. I let myself, turned on the lights, and pulled the curtains. The room was separated in three sections. The front had a couch with a lamp at each side and a TV on the dresser. The bathroom and closet were in the middle and the bed with another TV was in the back.

I put my luggage to the side and hooked up my computer. Instead of turning it on, I decided to go downstairs and get myself a drink. I left my hotel room and went down the elevator to the plaza. When I got there, I caught wind of what was going on before.

"That's fucking awesome, dude," one guy said.

"I can't believe she was in the same hotel as we were," another guy said.

"That's crazy," a third guy added.

The group excitedly headed out and went to the elevator. I shook my head and continued to the bar. An attendant was standing there with several bottles of wine and liquor stocked at the ready.

"Yes, sir," he said. "What would you like?"

"Get him a Merlot or a Zinfandel," I heard a woman say behind me. I turned to my left and saw it was Laura.

I laughed and then said, "According to the lady, I'm having a Merlot."

"You know her?" he asked. "She's a popular attraction here tonight."

"We went to high school together. Do you mind if I hug her before I get my drink?"

"That's fine with me, sir," he replied cheerfully.

I turned to her and wrapped my arms around her waist. She wrapped her arms around my shoulders and squeezed hard.

"So you were what all that commotion was about?" I said to her as I let go.

"They weren't expecting to see Megan Allen," she replied. "They came up and asked for a picture with me."

"Well, I bet they're heading back to their rooms to jerk off to you," I joked.

"Megan Allen fulfills a lot of fantasies," she said with a smile.

"Sir," the attended said as he handed me a glass. "Your wine."

"Thank you so much." I reached into my wallet, pulled out a five dollar bill for a tip, and placed it in the glass at the front of the bar.

"Thank you," he said. "You have a good evening."

"So what are you having?" I asked her.

"My glass is over there with Luther," she said, pointing at a table a few feet away. Luther raised up a peace sign as we made our way over to him.

"I remember you," he said. "You're Chris, right? You and Miss Allen went to high school together."

"That would be me," I replied. "I heard there was quite a commotion."

"Nah. They were cool. Courteous as hell. All I had to do was stand there and direct traffic. So what are you doing in Philly?"

"Regional meeting for work. I'm making a presentation to Philly and New Jersey reps. So what brings you to Philly?"

"Home base, my man. I run the business up here and my cousin handles things down in Virginia. But Miss Allen…she always gets personal protection from me."

"That's right," she said as they exchanged a fist bump. "I'll be a Club Risqué for the next couple nights. Then we are heading to New York City."

"Road warriors," I joked.

"Damn right," he said. Then his phone rang. He pulled it out of his pocket and said, "Hello…yeah…where is he supposed to be…that mother…" He took it off his ear and said to us, "I got an issue I need to handle."

"Luther, I'm fine," she said. "I'll be with Chris, so there's no issue here. Besides, I think we'll be heading to my room soon anyway." She looked at me and winked.

"I'll get her back to her room," I added.

He nodded to both of us and then headed off to continue his phone conversation.

Laura leaned over and whispered, "Let's get out of here." She got up from her seat and held out her hand for me. I obliged, and we walked from the plaza to the elevator. We got off at the fourth floor and went to her room. She opened the door, turned on the lights, and I took a seat on the couch. She closed the blinds at the front window, kicked off her shoes, and took a seat next to me.

"What's up with you besides the business trip?" she asked.

"You remember the last time you were in town?"

"How could I forget? That was quite a threesome experience. Michelle was something else."

"You told me she would refer me to someone else."

Laura laughed and then said, "I knew she would. A woman never forgets when she comes hard. How was her referral?"

"Good," I replied. "She liked being on her knees, if you know what I mean."

"Awesome!" she cheered. She raised her glass, and I returned the favor.

There was silence in the room as we savored our drinks. Then Laura started to rub her foot up and down my leg.

"What are you doing?" I asked.

"What do you think?" she cooed. "How about Round Three?" She maneuvered herself closer to me and tilted my head to hers. As she stroked her index finger up and down my cheek. I breathed heavily and sighed. I closed my eyes and winced.

"What's wrong, baby?" she asked.

"I...I can't," I answered. "I just can't."

"Why not? Why...oh," she quietly said. She moved a few inches away from me and sat in the middle of the couch. "Let me guess. It's Lisa."

"Yeah," I replied. "How did you..."

"I remember how you tripped out when I tried to get you to call her. I knew then you really liked her. So you want to date her?"

"She actually came by to see me, and I was upstairs fucking when she rang the doorbell."

"Did you let her in?"

"No. But she figured things out. She and I had a heated discussion about it, and she told me she didn't want to be a part of a rotation. She wanted to be with me and to not waste her time if I couldn't."

"So you're going for it?"

"Laura, I have to. I don't want to kick myself if she's the one, and I missed out because I'm trying to be Mr. Playboy. Look, you know..."

"I know," Laura assured me. "You and I will be friends no matter what. But it sounds like you need to go get your girl."

"Yeah," I replied. "Look, I'm going to turn in early. I've got a long day."

"No problem."

I got off the couch, and Laura followed me to the door. I turned around and she reached around my waist and gave me a big hug. I wrapped my arms around her shoulders and upper back and held her for a while.

"I love you," she whispered.

"I love you, too," I responded.

"I want a wedding invitation," she said as she let go of me.

"I haven't got there yet," I replied with a smile.

"You will." Then she leaned in and softly kissed me on the cheek. "You will."

I exited the room and took the adjacent stairs to the third floor and to my room. I opened the door and took a seat on the couch. I turned on the TV and there was a baseball game one. As I got comfortable, I pulled out my phone and sent a text to Lisa.

Hey, it's me. I'm in Philly tonight, and I'll be back in town tomorrow. I need to talk to you when I get back. There's something I need to say.

I sighed as I hit the Send button, wondering what may happen next. Then I got a response back from her.

Okay.

{ 48 }

My meeting with the Philadelphia and New Jersey teams
went better than expected. Everyone was pleased with what
I had put together in my regional reports. The only bad part
about the day was that it lasted longer than I intended. I
didn't leave Philadelphia until almost four in the afternoon,
which meant a long slog through traffic all the way home.

It didn't help matters that there was an accident in every
state I drove through. Each hour that passed by, I got more
anxious in my car. I desperately wanted to get to Richmond
but stopping and starting all through the interstate was not
helping. As I watched the sun dip from the sky and darkness
took over the landscape, doubt crept into my mind that I
would get there at a decent hour.

Just as traffic broke up and I had smooth sailing, it
started raining. A light rain turned into a heavy downpour as
I got into Virginia. That slowed down traffic once more, and
I pounded the steering wheel in frustration.

I didn't get into the Richmond area until ten in the evening. A thought of not going to Lisa's and just calling entered
my mind. Then I kept playing a scenario in my head of losing
any chance for her if I did. Going through this over and over
again was driving me crazy to the point that I pulled over at

an exit a few miles from home. I drove to a nearby truck stop and parked at the very back of the lot. I got out of my car and stood in the rain. I let the raindrops wet me from head to toe without a care.

I finally took a deep breath and got back in. I wiped my face and started up the car. As I got back on the interstate, I got a phone call on my cell. I looked and saw it was Lisa.

"I'm on the way," I said.

"Chris, it's getting late and I've got a long day tomorrow," she replied.

"Stay up," I pleaded. "I'm on the way."

"What's so damn important that it can't wait?"

"This can't wait, Lisa. If I wait, there may not be another chance to say it again."

"Chris," she replied with worry in her voice. "What's going on?"

"I need to talk to you...tonight. There's something that I need to say face to face. Stay up. Please."

"Okay," she relented. "How long are you going to be?"

"No more than twenty minutes. I promise."

"I'll be up," she sighed.

She hung up the call, and I let my end hang up on its own. I picked up speed and soon I found myself on a clear path down the interstate. Finally I pulled into her apartment complex and drove to her place. I parked my car and marched directly to her door. I knocked, and within seconds Lisa opened the door.

"Hey," she said.

I walked in without saying a word and took a seat on the couch. She looked at me with a puzzled look on her face as she took a seat on the other side of the couch.

"What is so damn important?" she asked sternly. "I haven't heard from you..."

"I know that," I replied. "I apologize but I had to clear my head."

"Clear your head of what?"

"Everyone. I needed to be away from everyone to figure out what the hell I'm trying to do. Ask some questions of myself and see where the answers lead me. And they're all leading me to one place."

"And what's that?"

"You." That last word stunned her and let her mouth wide open. "This is where I need to be."

"Chris,' she finally responded. "What are you saying?"

"I like you a lot, and you're right, you don't deserve to be in a rotation. You deserve to stand out on your own."

Lisa turned her head away, and it caught me by surprise. I reached over to her and put my hand on her shoulder. She turned to me with a smile on her face and tears in her eyes.

"I've been waiting for you to say that," she said as she held on to my arm. "I know I was hard on you on the basket-ball court and..."

"I deserved it," I replied.

"No, you didn't. We weren't an item, and I was jealous. I always wanted to come out on top."

"So you were competing for this?"

"Of course," she replied as she slid close to me. "I always like to compete." She kissed me and snuggled her head on my shoulder. "And I won. So what happens now?"

"We go where it takes us," I said. "No pressures, no expectations, but having a lot of fun doing it. Besides, we'll play again later in fantasy baseball. I wouldn't mind another steak dinner."

"Oh, fuck you," she replied as she perked up from her position. "You're gonna get your ass kicked next time."

"Whatever."

"But let's deal with that tomorrow. I need sleep and you need to get home."

"That's true," I said. I got up and headed to the front door.

"Hey," she said. "Thanks for keeping me up."

"It was worth it," I replied. "You're worth it."

I kissed her and gave her a big hug before walking out the door. When I got to my car, I saw her wave from outside the door. I waved back, got it, and drove off.

When I got home, I dumped my clothes in the hamper and put away my other stuff. As I was getting ready for bed, I remembered what Damon and I had talked about a while back about the book of numbers he gave me. I went into my bottom drawer and pulled it out. I took it downstairs to the kitchen and grabbed a trash bag out of one of the drawers.

"Damon, you're right," I said to myself. "You don't need this any more and neither do I."

{ 49 }

So Lisa and I became an item

It actually felt good because it made life a lot simpler. It reminded me of something a friend of mine told me about his marriage. He said the best part was that he knew where he needed to be and he knew where he needed to go.

I'm finding out he was right.

Lisa and I started going out to other events instead of just meeting up at the gym. We were out at an art gallery taking in a painting when I saw Sheila approach me. I introduced the two women and we made some small talk. Seeing Sheila again was great but the entire situation felt awkward. I watched her look at the way Lisa and I were holding hands and I sensed she wanted to know about us but didn't. Finally she asked if we were an item, and I told her yes. She nodded her head and congratulated us.

As she walked by us to another painting, she whispered to me, "Guess I'll have to save my keys for someone else."

It wasn't long after that that Melissa and Michelle cornered me one evening at the gym. Word had gotten around fast about Lisa and me dating. Both women had looks of anger on their faces and I wanted to get out of there as fast as I could. But then they both let up, telling me there were no worries or jealousy. I was a bit relieved at the whole thing and promised I wouldn't bring up our times together.

But there was one thing that Michelle wanted.

Lisa and I started taking her kickboxing class.

A few weeks later, I got a package in the mail from Laura. It was a DVD movie box cover where she was in this romantic pose with a guy. The title of the movie was called "The Reunion". She also had a note attached to the box.

Hey there.

Remember that script that I told you I was working on? Well, this is it. Getting together with you was great, and I just had to use that in a story. My friend Ryan wrote it with me and it's getting pretty good reviews so far. I hope you and Lisa are doing well. Remember, I want a wedding invitation!

Love you,

Laura

I ran into Lydia at the bookstore during the store's Summer Reading Kickoff event she set up for kids in the area. There were kids running all around the place, and there was an energy throughout the place that was infectious. Lydia and I talked briefly as one of the staff members was reading to the kids. She told me that Elle was coming back in town to do a concert and she really wanted to see me. The thought of that made me hesitate about the invitation. I told Lydia about Lisa and that we were an item.

She laughed and said, "So you're no longer dangerous?"

I replied, "I'll always be dangerous."

She laughed even louder and gave me a high five.

Lydia took it well, but Elle didn't. Her concert came up, and I took Lisa with me to see it. We ran into Elle before the show started, and I could see she was trying to hide her disappointment as I approached her with Lisa by my side. We greeted each other and Elle told us about her time in New York City and her preparation for her new album in the fall. But as I told her about Lisa and me, I could see this was not a topic that Elle wanted to hear. She cordially wrapped up our conversation, wished us well, and excused herself to the back.

The show was great. Elle gave a great performance, and I could see that Lisa was enjoying the performance.

At the end, Elle turned to her band and asked for a particular number. Then she turned to the crowd and said, "We're going to do one last number and I want to dedicate this to a former love. He and I shared some great times, and I was looking forward to seeing him again when I got back from New York. But he moved on and found someone else. I'm disappointed, but I'll be fine. I just want to wish him well. So this song is for him. It's called 'I Wish You Love'."

The sentiment made me take a deep sigh and I slouched in my seat. Lisa reached over to me and held my hand.

"That's for you, isn't it?" she whispered. I nodded my head and she rubbed my arm. She squeezed my hand tighter and rested her head on my shoulder throughout the song.

Finally, there is the fantasy league.

Lisa's team caught fire, and now she's in second place behind Danny. My team cooled off a little bit, but I'm right behind them in third. But that's okay. The season's not over with and there's enough time to catch both of them, and besides, Lisa and I have to play each other again.

Another chance to win a steak dinner.